DEPTH FINDER

Terry Paul Fisher

This book is dedicated to my brothers,
and to all the memories we share fishing on
the Racquet River.

And to my wife, Michelle, and my son Evan.
Thank you both for all your support and encouragement.

CHAPTER 1 / *The Canadian*

The Canadian rode in the passenger seat, uncertain of the young driver's ability to sneak him across the international border and into New York State tonight. He wasn't sure how they were going to cross, but after paying the owner of the truck five-thousand dollars, he was hopeful that it was money well spent. The fee had left him broke, but if everything went according to plan, he'd be a millionaire by this time tomorrow. If he could cross the St. Lawrence River, make it past the U.S. Border Patrol, and keep from being spotted by State Police, he could pull off a three-million-dollar heist with no witnesses.

They traveled in the cloak of darkness with the moon occasionally bouncing some light their way, but a winter storm was bearing down on the entire region and would soon obscure the moon and its glow. Some snowflakes were arriving early, bouncing off the windshield, as the western wind pushed the storm closer. The Canadian would use the storm for cover and take advantage of the quiet roads, as most drivers would be reluctant to be out.

The young Native-American driver lit a cigarette and cranked the window down a few inches. The wind sucked the smoke out of the truck as he exhaled.

"You running away from something, bro? Maybe a woman? A job?" the driver inquired.

"Does it matter?" the passenger answered.

"Hell no, it don't matter. You paid me good money to get your ass across the border, so I'm gonna get you across the border."

They rode the pothole-filled roads for another 15 minutes and entered the front wall of the storm. Large flakes, the size of dimes, drifted in the air and the driver was forced to turn on the wipers.

The truck smelled like motor oil, duct tape, and pizza. It reminded the Canadian passenger of his uncle's truck and the times he and his brother would sit on the bench seat, and they would all ride into the woods to go deer hunting. The V-8 engine under the hood had the same smooth purr, the interior vinyl was the same dark red, and the duct tape running front to back on the cracked seat was nearly in the same place. He would've bet money this was the same old Ford if he hadn't seen his uncle's truck after the wreck that killed him. Of course, the drunken asshole that hit him walked away from the accident with only a sprained wrist and bloody nose.

The truck was dark except for a few dashboard lights that shined blue on the young driver's face. An occasional draw from a cigarette illuminated the cab a little more.

"So, what's in the bag, bro?" the driver questioned.

The Canadian stared into the darkness beyond the hood and headlights of the truck without answering. His instincts forced him to keep a sense of direction, so he used the lights on a cell phone tower in the distance as a reference point. The falling snow had a dizzying effect on both the driver and the Canadian passenger, but it would obscure their entry into New York State.

The driver forced the conversation. "It don't matter to me. That's a pretty big bag in the back. I mean, if the cops see ya huffing with that, they're gonna run you down."

The passenger looked out the back window of the truck, but it was too dark to check on the bag.

"You best keep to the woods and back roads once I drop you off."

The Canadian knew the driver was right. Once they arrived in New York, he would need to acquire a vehicle. Staying on foot would draw attention from Border Patrol or State Police, and land him in jail or deported—probably both. Stealing a vehicle would be easy, but first, he needed to get across the border, which was no simple task in this area.

Northern New York was heavily populated by Border Patrol agents scouring back roads, highways, and parking lots in pursuit of illegal immigrants and drug dealers. Well-equipped agents were a curse to anyone trying to smuggle drugs, weapons, or people across the U.S./Canadian border, but the local smugglers were masters at evading the authorities. That's why the Canadian enlisted the services of this local twenty-two-year-old from the St. Regis Mohawk Reservation.

The reservation, locked between both nations, was the perfect place to cross from Canada into the United States illegally. But, it wasn't easy. Traveling at night meant risking your life. Traveling during the day meant risking your freedom. The smuggling routes were dangerous in the dark and varied from season to season.

High-speed boats could be heard crossing the St. Lawrence River during the early hours of spring and summer. They would ferry passengers or cargo through the waves, from one country to the other. When ice started covering the river in winter, snowmobiles were the vehicle of choice. Light and fast, the snowmobiles could cross the river in a few minutes. This was usually the most dangerous time to cross since it was difficult to tell where the ice was thin. Several people died every year trying to cross the ice on snowmobiles, determined to find a better life in the United States. Sometimes they made it—sometimes all they found was a terrible death, and their story was forgotten within a few days.

Once the ice had thickened to five inches, it would support a light truck and some cargo. A local gas station would advertise the thickness of the ice right in plain sight of the police and the public. The Fox Shop had an electronic sign to promote a cigarette brand that did not exist. If the price was three dollars per pack, then the ice was three inches thick. Once the price rose to five dollars, local smugglers knew it was safe to take their trucks across the ice-bridge. The false sign minimized conversations and questions about ice conditions but kept everyone informed.

Travis "Moonie" Swamp puffed on a cigarette as he drove the black F-150. He turned right and fishtailed down the snow-covered dirt road. Though the tires had lost their traction, Moonie maintained his composure and kept the vehicle on the road. He had driven this road at least once or twice a week for the last five years, often in winter conditions much worse than this. The Canadian was no stranger to the inclement weather himself and was unfazed by the truck's commotion. Moonie let off on the accelerator pedal, killed the headlights, and slowed the truck as they descended the dark, meandering road. They followed the fresh track from a snowmobile, barely visible by the ambient light of the night, letting it guide them like they were on a monorail. Six inches of fresh snow hid the gravel road that led them to the vast river ahead.

The sky had become completely overcast in the last ten minutes. Now, they were shielded from the light of the moon— invisible to the world. The only life watching them now was a thick row of white pines on each side of the road.

They rode the darkness for another two miles until the tall pines ended abruptly. The truck braked momentarily as they entered a vast clearing. The snowy field seemed to extend for eternity, fading into the abyss of the night. The Canadian could not see anything in front of him but darkness. The truck crawled from the woods, like a lion stepping into a field of zebras. Moonie eased the gas, and the truck crawled forward with a low growl. They turned to the right thirty-five degrees and came to a halt. Moonie turned off all the dashboard lights and tossed his stubby cigarette out the window. Then, he flicked his headlights on and off once. Five seconds passed, and he repeated the signal.

Finally, a light flashed back at them on the horizon.

"Here we go," Moonie said.

"This takes us to the river, eh?" The Canadian asked. He looked doubtful that Moonie meant to arrive at such an opening when they were trying to stay undetected.

Moonie smiled a goofy grin, shifted the black truck into four-wheel drive, and stomped the gas. Tires spun with a whirring sound that echoed through the truck bed. Once the Goodyears achieved traction, they accelerated across the open field.

"This doesn't take us to the river, bro," Moonie shouted over the roaring of the powerful V-8 engine. "This *is* the river!"

Four wheels clawed through white powder, ardently trying to grab the ice that supported the old Ford, thrusting it forward across the massive St. Lawrence River—forward in the darkness toward the state of New York. The ice below the wheels provided a smooth ride in contrast with the gravel road in the rearview mirror, but it came at the sacrifice of safety. As thick as the ice was, it still cracked and popped as the weight of their vehicle caused its brittle surface to bow. The Canadian's heart pounded, nervous from the speed and the noise, but anxious to keep their forward momentum, outrunning any cracks that may be forming in the vitreous road.

The Canadian's eyes adjusted to the low light. He gripped the handle above the door with enough strength to crush a tennis ball—his other hand on the dash and stiff legs braced him for the impact he thought was sure to come. He was not so much frightened for his life, but of the notion that an accident now would completely sabotage his agenda, and he would return to Canada as poor as when he awoke this morning.

The Canadian's tired eyes peered through a smoky windshield, searching for some structure or landmark he could lock onto as a reference to their navigation. A small light appeared in the distance. Moonie lightened his foot on the accelerator as he turned a couple of degrees to the right to correct his course. The Canadian's heart rate slowed with the decreasing speed of the truck. Both driver and passenger fixated on the light. The beacon waved back and forth, guiding the truck like a lighthouse guiding a ship on the Great Lakes.

When they arrived at the other shore, the Canadian was not happy to see a person standing on the edge of the river. He hoped there would be no witnesses to his illegal entry to the States. A young girl, presumably in her late teens, waved a small flashlight in their direction.

Moonie slowed the truck to a crawl as he approached the teen. The window of the truck descended into the door, letting the cold winter air enter.

"Good morning, sweetheart. Staying warm?"

The Canadian looked at the clock on the dash. 'Good Morning?' he thought. It was 11:00 p.m. They parked the truck on the solid ground, just 20 feet from the edge of the river. Moonie turned off the engine, and both passenger and driver got out.

The Canadian could barely see the girl in the night. She kept her head down even as she poked a small fire with a dry beaver stick. The fire grew a little with each taunting poke as air fed the hot coals. She smiled as the fire flared, and it brought her some security to shed light on the stranger's face. She had been there for five hours, alone in the dark, waiting for traffickers to pass. The dark was not her source of discomfort. Though she knew and trusted the locals that passed on her watch, she worried about the strangers that came through here seeking freedom, fortune, or glory. Sometimes they were rude or just crazy. Often, they were violent people who were fleeing from persecution. She had no shelter, no company, and no weapon, other than her phone with a nearly dead battery.

This was a job few were brave enough to do.

The Canadian looked around as they exited the truck. The fire was irresistible to both he and his guide. They both removed their gloves and gathered around the small fire, allowing the heat to penetrate their skin and warm chilled blood.

The girl did not make eye contact with the passenger. She talked softly, holding her arms close to her body, sheltering herself as young girls do while in the presence of an unfamiliar man. The Canadian dismissed the posture as just someone trying to keep herself warm, but Moonie could sense her discomfort immediately. She was uneasy about the red-bearded man's presence, so Moonie decided that as much as he wanted to stay and talk with the pretty girl, their stop would be brief.

There was no imminent danger, but she had heard stories of girls gone missing while performing this duty in the past. Being the beacon on the "Ice Bridge" was a dangerous occupation. Hypothermia, drowning, and being murdered were all very real consequences of guiding unlawful travelers across the vast darkness of the St. Lawrence River. But it was also a necessary job that paid very well. One night of standing in the dark, flagging smugglers across with her flashlight, paid more than any minimum wage job could in a whole week. The reward outweighed the risks, save for the half-dozen people who'd gone missing over the years. Most were never found and existed now only in memory. Those who were found had an autopsy report that listed the cause of death as either hypothermia or a gunshot wound.

"How's the border looking, Kim?" Moonie asked the young girl.

Kim looked up from the orange flames. For the first time, the Canadian could see her face. Kim's smooth skin seemed to glow in the firelight. Her brown eyes, almost as warm as the fire itself, glanced at the Canadian and then back to Moonie.

"Everything looks clear on the U.S. side. Brian and Otter came through about an hour ago with no trouble. Friend of mine said there was a bad accident that had most of the badges busy for the night. Maybe a fatality."

"Brian and Otter? What are those bozos up to?"

"Don't know, but they did say the south side is breaking up close to shore. Sun was too warm today. Be careful, Moonie. Hate to see that nice truck drop in the drink."

Moonie laughed. "Thanks for the love, sweetheart. Don't worry, we'll get through. We best be going before you start falling in love with me or something." He reached into his pocket and pulled out a small bundle of cash, separated a couple of $20 bills and gave them to Kim. A tip, the Canadian guessed.

Kim smirked as she took the money. "Thanks. I'll see you on the way back."

"Don't start missing me and try to follow," Moonie joked.

"Hold me back, eh," Kim joked. She looked over at the impatient Canadian. Kim's smirk vanished as she turned from his cold demeanor to face the warm fire. Moonie placed a log on the fire, relieving Kim of the burden. The fire sparked, and smoke drifted into her face, forcing her to close her eyes tight and hold her breath. When she finally looked up again, Moonie and his fare were back in the truck.

"What did she mean by the 'south side is breaking up?'" the burly Canadian asked while Moonie lit a cigarette.

"Oh, don't worry about that, bro. She just meant the ice is breaking up a little by the shore. We'll have to drive through a little water on the other side of the river."

"Didn't we just cross the river?" the Canadian asked.

"That was the first part of the river. Right now, we're on an island. The next section of the river is just ahead."

They didn't take long to cross the short stretch of land, and the Canadian was surprised to see a few house lights in the area, indicating that people lived on this little island. The lights gave him a sense of direction, and he welcomed that. The snow around the lights illuminated, giving the lights a beautiful glow that reminded him of the hockey rink he used to skate on as a child. The road descended, and within minutes they were putting the tires on the ice again.

The Canadian peered through the frosty windshield and noticed the trees gave way to another opening of snow as flat as a sheet of paper. The only trace of the path they were to follow was faded tire tracks from Brian and Otter's truck that traversed the river just 60 minutes prior. The relentless snow falling had already made the tire tracks difficult to see.

Moonie's truck set sail across the opening, accelerating over the ice. The distance between the two shores was shorter than the previous. Moonie drove slower this time, perhaps because this stretch of the river seemed to be hidden. There was a sharp curve in the riverbank that obscured the view from shore, hiding them a little more than the previous river channel. The tall pines on the other side gave them cover and muffled the sound of the engine as they drove south and then turned 20 degrees to the west, cutting across the frozen river diagonally. They made it across in less than two minutes.

Moonie slowed the truck to a crawl as they approached the open water that appeared between them and the U.S. shore. The truck tracks in the snow dropped off the ice and into the open water near shore. The Canadian ran a hand through his red beard while he studied the broken ice. He turned to Moonie. "Think it's safe, eh?"

Moonie studied the broken ice himself. "No problem, bro. The water's only about two feet deep there."

"You sure about that?" the Canadian asked.

"Sure, I'm sure. My brother and I fish for walleye on this part of the river. We always stay away from this area, so we don't break the prop on his Jon boat."

The Canadian felt no safer. He closed his brown eyes and let his mind drift for a moment. He envisioned a large headstone amid a green field with flowers adorning the sides. The surface was polished like the marble counters in the bank to contrast with the engraved letters which were course and deep. A lone figure stood weeping, as still as a tall oak tree adjacent to the plot. The oak cast a dark shadow over the fresh grave. The Canadian reached out and started to whisper a name...

Moonie interrupted the thought. "No turning back now, eh, bro."

He shifted the truck into first gear and crept up to the edge. The front tires dropped into the water—more ice broke—then Moonie hit the gas hard. The rear wheels spun on the glassy ice while front wheels pawed at the bottom of the river. With the headlights pointing down and the rear of the truck elevated, the Canadian could see the water turn cloudy with mud. The truck lurched forward, dropping completely into the river, submerged to the running boards. The distance was only 15 feet from broken ice to shore. They ascended out of the cold water and up the steep embankment. The tires slung mud in every direction while the engine spewed steam. The Canadian relaxed his grip on the dash and noticed the satisfying smile on Moonie's face.

"See, bro? No problem. Welcome to New friggin' York," Moonie said.

"Thank you, Jesus," the Canadian muttered under his breath. He had enough of the rough ride, the blackness, and of his uneducated companion. This is where they would part ways. Moonie drove the truck for another two miles before stopping along a row of thick cedars. Towering over the cedars were large utility structures that carried electricity from the St. Lawrence River to New York City—a journey of approximately 300 miles. The towers hummed as the electrical current traversed the copper wire at the speed of light.

The Canadian realized why this place was so barren of homes or businesses. The powerful electrical lines were not only an eye-sore, but most likely the cause for a lot of cancer in the region. Why would anyone want to live close to these?

They both stepped out and listened for approaching vehicles. Silence.

The Canadian stood with his face in the wind. He felt the snowflakes pelting his cheeks and eyelids. The cold was like a fresh cup of coffee, awakening his senses. The first leg of his journey was complete, and nothing should stop him from reaching his goal. He could almost smell the dirty money and imagined how it would feel to hold it in his hands.

The storm that was forecasted was bearing down on them now. The wind became noticeably stronger, and the snow began to form drifts.

He moved to the back of the truck, lowered the squeaky tailgate, and pulled on his large backpack. It slid across the plastic bed liner with ease. He turned to hoist the pack onto his shoulders but stopped when he realized Moonie was pointing a 9 mm pistol at his forehead. He let out a quick, short sigh as if the young Native American was annoying him. The Canadian stayed calm, not wanting to make the nervous young man react.

"What the hell, Moonie?"

"I said I'd get you across the border. Now...whatever's in that bag seems pretty valuable, bro. Leave the bag in the back of the truck and start walking."

"Seriously? You're going to rob me after I just paid you five grand?"

"Sorry, bro, but a man's got to make a living," Moonie responded. "All you gotta do now is keep walking south. Follow these power lines until you get to a smaller river. Follow the smaller river upstream until you meet the highway. Where you go from there...well, I don't give a shit." Moonie laughed. "Good luck."

"I'm not leaving here without this backpack," the Canadian assured him.

"Dude! Do you not see the fuckin' gun in your face?" Moonie tightened his grip and turned the gun sideways for effect. The Canadian realized Moonie had no idea how to handle the weapon and was imitating some shit he'd seen in the movies. Turning the gun was a big mistake. Moonie's wrist was no longer supinated, which reduced mobility in the joint.

"Set the bag down," Moonie ordered. He pushed the gun within inches of the Canadian's forehead—another big mistake.

The Canadian's hands moved in a blur, timed perfectly with a head feint to the right. Before Moonie could realize what was happening, the Canadian's right hand came left, grabbing the slide of the pistol. His left forearm came up as the right hand pulled the gun down. The force of the burly forearm against the thin wrist broke the pistol from Moonie's hand instantly, and a half-second later Moonie was staring down the barrel of his own gun.

"Whoa, bro, take it easy. I wouldn't have pulled the trigger. The thing's not even loaded, okay?"

"Then why are you about to piss your pants?"

There was nothing for the Canadian to say. His stare was colder than the northwest wind blowing in Moonie's face. The wind gusted up to 30 miles per hour as if the Canadian's rage controlled its speed. Moonie's eye's watered from the stinging cold, but he was too scared even to blink. The wind gust dissipated, and the Canadian took a deep breath. "How much gas is in the truck?"

"Uh…gas…I think…I don't know…maybe…"

"How much fucking gas is in the truck?" the Canadian interrupted.

"Quarter of a tank. May…maybe more," Moonie said.

"Is there a road out to the highway?"

"Yeah," Moonie replied. He was starting to get his hopes up. Maybe the Canadian would have him drive him to the highway. "This road goes all the way. It's a private road, but the owner keeps it plowed," he was talking as fast as the gust of wind. "We can make it to the highway in about ten minutes."

"We? You're going to have a nice walk home, asshole."

"Yeah, yeah, I'll just walk, bro. You take my truck," he was backing up to the driver's side door, which he'd left open the entire time. "Let me grab my coat, okay? I'll freeze to death if I don't take it."

The Canadian's stare was frigid. "Get your coat then, and get the hell out of here."

Moonie went into his truck halfway. His feet stayed in the snow as he leaned into the F-150. The Canadian finished buckling the straps on the backpack when he heard a noise come from within the truck—metal on metal—the distinct sound only a former commando would recognize—a shotgun barrel.

The Canadian's hand rocketed upward, popping off the safety of the pistol, as Moonie spun with a 12-gauge shotgun in hand. The young smuggler had to step back so he could swing the shotgun around, but the movement to let the gun barrel clear the

17

truck was slow and clumsy. The desperate act took far too long and was no match for the speed of the trained former soldier. The Canadian shot without even looking down the pistol's sights. The force of the lead knocked Moonie against the truck door, which sprung a little, and pushed him back. He fell forward and sideways and landed in a puff of snow.

"Sonovabitch!" the Canadian blurted. "Why the hell didn't you just go? How could you be so stupid?"

Moonie gasped to catch his breath. The ballistic force of the bullet had knocked the wind out of his lungs. He felt little pain; just the cold of the snow on his shoulders and neck. The Canadian pulled his gloves from his pockets, wiped off the pistol, dumped the magazine, and gave it a toss like a broken boomerang.

"I'm sorry, kid. Really, I am. It didn't have to be this way. You've got balls; I respect that. But this time, you fucked with the wrong guy."

The thin Mohawk lay on the cold ground unable to move, looking to the sky. He was fully aware of everything happening around him. The bullet had mushroomed on impact, tearing a golfball size hole in his liver before severing his spine. The last thing he heard was the door of his truck slam closed and the tires spinning frozen gravel.

His breath came back to him, but not for long.

Chapter 2 / *Paul & Stacie*

Snow had been silently accumulating for the last six hours at a rate of an inch an hour. It had stopped now. The Arctic jet stream had finished dumping the white precipitation and quietly advanced to the East. The moon's light sparkled off little crystals in the fluffy snow, illuminating Paul's driveway enough that he could shovel without any artificial light. He stopped shoveling the snowdrifted driveway to admire the early morning sky populated with too many stars to count. His lungs filled with the cool winter air as he sucked it through his nostrils and held it deep for a few seconds. The rush of oxygen energized him, and tired muscles were revived and ready for the second half of the 70-foot long drive. His shovel dug in, pushing snow to the outer edges. The work was arduous but necessary. Beads of sweat formed on his brow, as his body temperature rose. There was only one place he would have rather been, and he would be there in about two hours.

Normally, the highway department would have been out clearing the streets at this time. Their massive plows made short work of the plugged streets, pushing snow in waves of white powder. However, today was a holiday—the first day of the year, and all the town employees were home sleeping off the previous night's celebration. Paul Marten had skipped the ball dropping and booze to get some rest. It was 4:00 in the morning, and he was to meet his brother Jack at 6:00. Only the waxing gibbous moon watched him work until the light mounted above the garage flashed on, illuminating the ground almost all the way to the road. A curvy silhouette stood in the window of the front door. She peeled back a curtain and gave a little wave. Paul waved back to his wife.

She disappeared, and then the bathroom window lit up. Paul knew she was hitting the shower and getting ready for work.

Paul pushed and scraped until all the snow had been piled high on each side of the driveway. Then he cleaned the snow from around his mailbox, even though there would be no mail service today. When his chore was complete, he put the shovel in the garage and headed back into the house. The curvy silhouette brought him a hot cup of coffee as a reward.

"Thanks, hon," Paul said as he took the cup.

Stacie knew that he was shoveling the driveway for her sake since his four-wheel drive truck would easily escape the snow's depth. The kiss on the cheek was all the thanks he needed, but the coffee was nice, too.

"Thank *you*," Stacie smiled. She was wearing nothing but a white bath towel.

"Don't thank me…it's my job," Paul replied as he hugged the bath towel. Stacey's warm body gave into Paul's grasp, letting herself be squeezed until his right hand caressed her bare left shoulder.

"Agh…you're freezing!" Stacey shrieked. "Keep your cold hands to yourself."

She pecked his cheek and marched back up the stairs to dress for work. Stacie usually left for work before Paul was awake. Her job as a security screener at Bettinger Airport required her to clock in at 5:30 a.m. and it was a 30-minute commute. She would be leaving in 40 minutes to make it on time, which was just enough time to do her hair and makeup.

When she came back down, she was wearing dark blue slacks, a medium blue shirt adorned with badges, and a name tag that read "S. Marten." She then slipped on a bulky winter coat that hid her figure much more than the towel had.

"Not having breakfast?" Paul questioned the spunky blonde. She held up a banana to answer his question and slid it into the coat's pocket.

"I hate going out in this cold," she complained as she struggled to wrap her arms around Paul. The coat restricted her movement, but she pushed the seams close to breaking to feel him close. "Why don't we sell this house, and move someplace warmer? Someplace where there's night life, and jobs, and more people than cows."

"Maybe someday," Paul said softly. He knew, financially, they may have to sell the house anyway, before they were forced into foreclosure. They were late on this month's mortgage, and he'd been out of work for six weeks. The financial strain had been taking its toll lately. Paul seemed to be agitated all the time, trying to find a decent job as an I.T. Manager.

Stacie knew it was a moot discussion. She had been making the suggestion every winter for the last four years. She glanced at the top of the hutch and saw a half dozen swim trophies Paul had won in college. The other eight were packed away in the attic. He was a gold-medalist swimmer and only lost the state championship by five-hundredths of a second. "We could find a place with a nice pool, and you could swim every day," she propositioned, trying a new sales pitch.

"Would you swim with me?"

"Maybe."

"Hmmm, might be worth it to see you in a bikini every day."

She laughed and finally ended the embrace. "Maybe if I keep going to the gym every week, but since we can't afford that, I'll just stick to my one piece."

Paul reached for his coffee sitting on the kitchen table and nearly spilled the cup. He shuffled through a half-dozen bills that laid on the table with his other hand. Stacie had paired several checks and bills with pink paperclips and adorned their envelopes with left-over Christmas stamps. Three of the bills were overdue and were absent of the pink paperclip and the accompanying check.

"Do these need to be mailed today?" Paul asked.

Stacie saw the concern on Paul's face. It crushed her that they could not pay their bills on time. Since he'd been laid off from the paper mill, they'd only received one unemployment check. "No mail today, remember? It's a holiday."

"Oh…. Maybe I shouldn't go fishing, today. I could make a few phone calls and—"

"No, don't you dare back out on your brothers. You guys have been planning this since Thanksgiving. Go. Have fun. Your brothers are good at making you laugh, and you need to have a little fun," she demanded.

"I know, but I should be—"

She cut him off again with a hand gesture.

"Stop it," she demanded. "Don't feel so guilty about taking a fun day. You've been looking for work for four weeks. You're not going to find a job today. Besides, no one else is working today, so why should you? What about the other option we talked about last week—starting your own business?"

"I'd love to do that," he leaned back on the counter and stared at the ceiling. "But, I'd need start-up capital. I would need money for software and equipment, a business license, business cards, a web domain, and advertising."

"So? You could get a small business loan."

"Maybe, but with all of the bills being late for the last month. What bank is going to take the chance of giving me a loan? Even if they did, my interest rate would be sky high."

"Talk to the bank and find out what they can do for you. Then we'll make the decision."

Paul knew how much faith Stacie had in him. It could take years to make a profit with his own business. Still, it was his dream. He pushed the dream aside and straightened forward. "You're going to be late. You should get on the road."

With that, the conversation was over. Paul knew she was right. He'd done all he could to find work, and there was little he could do today to improve their situation. Today, he needed to take his mind off their problems and go fishing. Monday afternoon he'd go to the local bank and talk to them about a possible loan.

"Be careful driving into work," Paul advised as he turned toward the coffee maker. "The state highway might be plowed, but

I know the town boys have the morning off. Secondary roads won't be plowed until this afternoon."

Paul poured another coffee into a travel mug for his hour-long drive while Stacie laced on her boots. He then started packing a small cooler from the garage. Four bottles of water, two beers, a package of Glazier hotdogs, an apple, and a few protein bars filled the cooler. He needed buns for the hotdogs, but he could purchase those at the store where he was meeting Jack and Eric.

Stacie finished lacing her boots and stood up to greet her husband one more time. The boots made her seem two inches taller now. She picked up a lunch bag and a laptop and made her way across the kitchen to give her husband one more kiss. He took the kiss, and the laptop bag from her hands and walked her to her car parked in the garage.

"Okay," commented Paul. "I won't be home until after dark—maybe around eight."

"Take your time and have fun. And be careful," Stacey demanded.

"I'm always careful."

Stacey rolled her eyes as the corners of her mouth turned upward. "You are the complete opposite of careful, Mr. Marten. Do you have everything you need?"

"Yes, Dear," replied Paul. "I'm even wearing clean underwear just in case I'm in an accident."

She punched his arm. "Good luck. See you tonight."

"Thanks. Have a great day."

Stacie climbed into her car, pushed the button to open the garage door and drove out into the cleanly shoveled driveway. Her commute to Bettinger International Airport would take 35 minutes. The morning flight was scheduled to depart at 5:50 am, and she needed to be there early enough to screen its seven passengers. She didn't like her schedule. She liked her job even less. Safeguarding passengers and planes since 9/11 lured her to work for the Department of Homeland Security several years ago. However, at an airport this small her impact was minimal. Stacie dreamed of working in a place where she could make a difference in people's lives, and she knew an airport with only 30 passengers a day was not that place.

"Why am I doing this?" she thought to herself. "Why do I keep working this fucking job?" She was talking to the pretty girl in the rearview mirror, but over her shoulder, standing in the driveway, was the tall, handsome answer to her question. Her smile returned momentarily, and she forced a positive thought to extinguish her doubts. She thought about how much she loved Paul. She thought about how much she was looking forward to their lives together. She thought about how he would react when she told him she was pregnant. She placed her hand on her belly, imagining what she would look like in a few more months.

Paul watched his young wife accelerate out of sight. He needed to finish loading his truck with gear and looked to the sky once again. The stars were still shining, and the moon was setting over the neighbor's field. Three deer were silhouetted in the moonlit snow. They shuffled toward an old oak tree, poking their noses in the white fluff looking for Fall's remaining acorns. None to be found, they turned north and walked toward a neighbor's apple orchard, hoping a few winter apples had finally lost their hold from the upper branches. The smallest of the three limped on his rear leg but managed to keep up with the other two. Paul watched until they ducked into the shadows of the basswood trees. His eyes scanned the sky one more time. A yellow ray of light on the horizon was starting to lift the dark sky. The sun would be up soon, and Paul had to meet Jack and Eric before sunrise. He loaded his sled full of gear into the back of his Dodge, cranked the engine, and spun out of the driveway.

Chapter 3 / *The Marten Brothers*

Jack Marten stood in line at the counter of the little convenience store in the heart of Higley. It was a humble little store with narrow rows of canned goods, junk food, camping supplies, and even a couple shelves of hardware items. Two outdated gas pumps occupied the small parking lot where campers, hunters, and loggers, would wait in turn to fill their vehicles with the most expensive fuel within a 20-mile radius.

The building was built when Jack's father was just a boy, and he would tell stories about the original owner who operated a poker tournament in an empty storage room at the back of the building. The local authorities were regular players in the games until the town supervisor's intoxicated daughter was taken there and raped one night. The owner went to prison, and the building was abandoned for nearly 30 years. No one living in Higley could afford to purchase the commercial building until years of abandonment had taken its toll on the value of the property. A local kid, who had flunked out of community college, bought the property with his inheritance money and was now building a second store on the south side of town.

The store opened at 5:00 a.m., which wouldn't make sense in most neighborhoods across the state. But, the little store catered to the loggers, and they started their workday by 6:00 a.m. Today, the store would be open early for the fishermen. Some were there for snacks and beverages; some were shopping for fishing supplies and minnows; a few were there for lottery tickets and cigarettes, but almost everyone was purchasing gas.

27

The store would normally be booming on a Saturday morning, but today was quieter than usual. Jack figured most of the fishermen were running late and dealing with their hangovers.

Jack tapped his right thumb against his thigh as he stared impatiently at the clock. He was an impatient man, especially when it came time to go fishing or hunting. This morning, he and his brothers would drive south 45 miles to their favorite ice-fishing spot. The earlier they arrived, the better their chances of catching the northern pike that dwelled in the bays. He adjusted the groceries in his left arm while waiting in the short line at the counter. The customer in front of him was a mountain of a man. He stood about six and a half feet tall with broad shoulders and thick forearms. He was venting to the cashier about his stolen jeep. His voice was hoarse and deep from years of screaming over the sound of chainsaws and wood chippers. He spoke loudly with a raw tone and a frank manner. Jack was anxious to get out of the store and get back on the road. He wanted to tell the other customer to hurry his ass up. He would have, too, if Paul had been on time. But, as usual, Paul was running late.

Jack's thumb tapped a little faster.

"Com'on," Jack thought to himself. "Nobody gives a shit about your piece-of-shit Jeep. Some of us have plans today." He stared at the back of the big man's head, trying to will the thoughts telepathically so the man would leave. It didn't work.

"...and then, when I came out of the bar," the tall customer was explaining to the cashier, "my damn Jeep was gone, and I had to call the ol' lady to come get me. Talk about an ass-chewing."

The cashier laughed, "Holy shit, man. And she didn't even know you were at the bar?"

"Nope. She thought I was still working downstate where they had the ice storm."

"So, did you call the sheriff?"

"Hell yeah, I called the fucking sheriff," the mountain continued. "They found a stolen truck in the parking lot, too. They figure some guy stole the truck from the Reservation, drove it this far, then ditched it at the bar and made off with my Jeep."

The cashier shook his head in disbelief. "Oh man, you never friggin' know these days. I hope they find it in one piece."

"I hope I find the little bastard first. He'll wish he'd never even looked at my Jeep."

The cashier handed him his bag, "Good luck, Toady."

"Toady?" Jack thought to himself. The name suited the man with the croaky voice.

Jack was starting to feel some sympathy for Toady. Losing your vehicle in this part of the state would be like living on an island with no boat—you'd be stranded. He checked on his truck sitting in the parking lot. Still there.

"Good morning, Jack" the plump cashier faked a smile.

"Good?" Jack asked. "It's a great friggin morning." The excitement and anticipation of the day were too much for Jack to hold back. No work today, just a full nine or ten hours on the ice. He set down a package of cheese curd, two soda bottles, and some beef jerky. Door chimes diverted Jack's attention in the direction of the entrance as Paul entered. He was 12 minutes late, but that was no surprise to Jack.

"Good morning," Paul nodded to his brother and the cashier.

"Good morning," replied the cashier. His head was tilted down so he could see over the thin reading glasses resting on his nose.

"You're late," replied Jack to his sibling.

"Yeah, I had to make sure Stace could get out of the driveway. She needed to go to work this morning."

"She still works on Saturdays?" Jack asked. "I thought she was going to quit that job."

"She'd like to, but she can't until I get back to work," Paul said. "That might be months away since the economy's going to shit around here."

The 20-something-year-old cashier nodded in agreement.

"Hey, you need anything? I'm buying," Jack asked his younger brother.

"Just some hot dog buns," Paul responded.

"And a bag of hot dog buns," Jack said to the cashier.

The cashier rang up the groceries, stuffed everything in a paper bag, and took a 50 dollar bill from Jack's hand. "Don't forget your buns," he reminded as he handed back the change.

The two brothers left the store after grabbing the bag of buns and made their way to the trucks. A tall, lanky figure was standing at the back of Jack's truck. He was taller than Paul and Jack, with longer hair and a three-day beard. His face had many of the same characteristics as Paul's and Jack's. Eric was the youngest of the three brothers. Barely old enough to drink alcohol legally, he was six years younger than Paul and nine years behind Jack. Paul hadn't noticed Eric was sitting in Jack's truck when he pulled into the parking lot. He was happy to see his younger brother and glad he was joining them for the day.

"Hey, what's new?" Paul asked Eric as they shook hands.

"Not too much. I start my new job on Monday—working at the college," Eric replied.

"Finally going to college, huh?" Paul joked.

Eric laughed, "Well, until they kick me out."

Eric had never gone to college but was as smart as anyone Paul knew. When Eric finished high school, he had several scholarships to attend various technical schools. Instead, he opted to go to work in their uncle's garage, working on foreign cars. He preferred to learn by getting his hands dirty. Eric could take an engine apart and put it back together by the time he was fifteen. He learned everything their farther could teach them about engines and mechanical devices. While most kids were off with friends on the weekends, Eric spent Friday and Saturday nights in the garage. Sometimes he was joined by a few friends, but usually, it was just some father and son time.

"Did you get into the maintenance department?" Paul asked.

31

Eric nodded. "I'll be working on all of their trucks, lawnmowers, and other vehicles. I'll miss Uncle Floyd's garage, but this job has full benefits and retirement. I can't pass that up."

"No, you can't," Paul said. He was happy for Eric, but deep down felt a little jealous. Paul had been searching for a good job for weeks. He and Stacie were burning through their savings, and things were starting to look bleak.

Eric's new opportunity came from one of Floyd's satisfied customers. The customer happened to be the maintenance supervisor at Clarkson University. She was impressed by the service she received when her Toyota 4-Runner lost its transmission, so she offered Eric a job the next week.

"I tried calling you Wednesday," Paul nodded to Eric.

"Oh, I was probably at a meeting," Eric replied.

"I didn't know you were still going to those," Paul noted.

"Well, I don't have to anymore. Now it's optional, so I go once in a while," Eric explained. "It just helps me when I'm stressing out and feel like I need a drink."

Paul wanted to change the subject. He knew Eric felt bad about his former drinking problem and didn't want to upset him. They were supposed to enjoy the day, just three brothers hanging out in the remote Adirondack wilderness, catching some fish—hopefully.

"Enough chit-chat. Let's hit the highway, boys." Jack urged. "Can't catch anything in this parking lot."

Jack transferred his fishing gear to Paul's truck. They moved large plastic sleds, a couple of pack baskets filled with tip-ups, an ice auger for drilling holes, a small chainsaw, and a cooler. The brothers climbed in and buckled up. Their destination was another 40 miles south, and the sky reminded them that they were running out of darkness.

They preferred drilling holes before the sun came up to increase their odds of catching a morning walleye. When the walleye stopped feeding, the northern pikes would awake and stalk the shallow bays to satisfy their voracious appetites. The Marten brothers would be there, too, with fresh minnows, metal hooks, and steely determination.

They drove through town, waving to a few elderly gentlemen out shoveling their driveways and sidewalks, wondering if that would be them someday. Would they stay here and tolerate the long winters and the icy economy? Or, would they ever be compelled to make a life somewhere that had a traffic light? Only time held the answer to that question.

They loved their hometown. Higley was a place where everybody knew your name—perhaps even your middle name. It was a residential town, with no college, no factories, no big office buildings, and few jobs. Most adults had to commute to neighboring towns for employment.

Higley was nestled in the foothills of the Adirondack Mountains and was the largest town —in square miles—in the entire state of New York. It was also one of the smallest towns based on population. The town was formed around a furniture factory and a sawmill in the early 1800s. The logs were cut by hand along the mountains and floated down the river to the sawmill. Once cut, the lumber was taken to the furniture factory or shipped downstate for a price. All of that was put to a halt when the state decided the river would be a perfect place to install three hydroelectric dams. The dams caused the river to flood roads, homes, and some businesses, and the town was restructured around the river.

The Raquette River, which flowed north into the St. Lawrence River, split Higley right down the middle. The west side of the river was more developed than the east. Traveling on the east side of the river was only possible in a four-wheel drive vehicle, snowmobile, or ATV via a vast network of gravel roads and trails. Hunting camps were sporadically located along the river and throughout the vast boreal forest, with limited access, dependent on the season and the weather. Only three bridges spanned the Raquette River, allowing vehicles to traverse from one side to the other. The bridges were not close in proximity to one another, but rather, spread over 60 miles. The Marten brothers would drive to the most southern bridge and fish in an area they called Bear Bay.

Paul leaned on the driver-side door, steering the Ram truck south on Route 56. Jack had jumped in the back seat of the crew-cab truck, allowing Eric to occupy the shotgun seat, which gave him access to the tuner on the radio. He started thumbing preprogrammed buttons, dissatisfied with his choices.

"Don't like my stations?" Paul asked Eric.

"Sorry, but your hard-rock gives me a headache. And, who listens to NPR?"

"I do. So do a lot of people. It's informative and educational," Paul retorted.

"It's boring."

"It can be," Paul started to explain to his younger brother, "but it can help you think about things...look at topics from a new perspective, and sometimes make you change your mind about important stuff."

"Maybe I can find the weather."

"I caught the weather last night," Jack said. "Light snow shower on and off all day. It's going to be overcast all day. High around 30 degrees."

"Sounds perfect," Paul said. "What about the storm that's coming?"

"That should stay north of where we're going, but it will hit town in about an hour or two. It's only expected to last until early afternoon. Should be clear by the time we get off the ice."

"Awesome. Let's go get some fish," Eric exclaimed. He spun the tuner dial until the digits on the screen read 99.5. A Jason Aldean song came through the speakers, and soon, all three brothers were quietly singing along.

They drove south for another 11 miles. The road meandered up and down the foothills, increasing their elevation to 1,600 feet. If they had driven another eight miles, they would have come to the lake where the Raquette River was born. They turned left and crossed the last bridge that spanned the river. Once on the east side, they turned right onto Garrison Road and maintained their journey along the opposite side of the river.

Paul powered off the radio that now seemed to be stuck between stations. The radio waves were lost in the vast Adirondack forest, and the sound was more static than music. Then he switched off the truck's headlights.

"Look's like someone beat us here," Paul stated.

Jack sat up and leaned between the two front bucket seats. He could see tracks on the snow-covered road that were made after last nights squall. He studied them for a few seconds. "Those tracks are a few hours old. Narrow vehicle. Aggressive tread."

Jack worked for the town highway department and drove hundreds of miles every week in conditions similar to this. He had followed almost every kind of vehicle track on these dark, snowy roads. He and his wingman, who operated the plow's height and angle, would play a guessing game whenever they saw tracks in the road. When you had nothing else to look at for hours during a plow run, playing "Guess the Tracks" was the only way to occupy your mind and pass the time. Usually, the tracks turned into someone's driveway, and the make and model of the track-making vehicle would be revealed.

"Those are Jeep tracks," Jack stated plainly. Paul and Eric knew better than to question his deduction.

"Well, looks like we'll have company today," Eric mused.

"I don't think so—look," Paul pointed out the windshield to a green Jeep Renegade parked in the middle of the road. He stopped the truck 30 yards from the vehicle, blocking the access road. Jack could see a custom decal on the back window—a cartoon frog wearing a plaid shirt and holding a chainsaw.

"Toady," Jack mumbled.

Paul and Eric looked at their older brother with skewed eyebrows. Jack could feel their confusion.

"There was a logger in the store this morning. Someone stole his Jeep last night from the bar," Jack explained. "I heard the cashier call him 'Toady.'"

"Shit," said Eric. "Well, it's probably some teenage kids screwing around."

The back door of Paul's truck opened, and Jack jumped out. Paul and Eric looked at each other and decided they better follow. Jack was already halfway to the abandoned vehicle. The windows were frosted over, indicating that the vehicle was cold and had been turned off for about two hours. Jack approached from the driver's side, using the side mirror to look inside. Paul and Eric jogged up from behind to catch up to their older brother.

Jack knocked on the side of the Jeep to get the attention of anyone who might be sleeping off a hangover. No response. He knocked one more time. Nothing.

The vehicle was abandoned, and a set of footprints led away from the parked Jeep. The tracks indicated that someone had exited the driver's side, gone to the back of the Jeep, and then hiked straight into the woods.

"Think it was someone grabbing their ice fishing gear?" Paul asked.

"No," Jack answered, rubbing his beard. "They headed uphill." He pointed to a high ridge to the left of the road. "If they were going fishing, he would've gone west, toward the river."

Eric nodded his head in agreement. "Well, we can't wait for him to come back." He opened the creaky door of the 4x4 and looked inside. "Ha! Keys are in the ignition." He climbed inside and started the six-cylinder engine, let out the clutch, drove it forward, and parked to the side of the road, giving Paul enough room to get his truck past. Before he exited the vehicle, Eric peeked at the backseat. There were piles of empty energy drinks and fast food wrappers on the floor. A snow-scraper on the seat, a muddy pair of work boots, and a chainsaw wrench.

Half folded on top of everything, was a geographical map of the area. Red marks had bled through to the back side of the map, and Eric's curiosity got the best of him. Maybe this would explain where the mystery driver went. He unfolded the map completely and studied it for a moment. The road to this point was highlighted all the way down from the Canadian border. A black line, drawn with a straight edge, was drawn on the map. It started somewhere in Canada, which was not certain since this was a New York map. Little arrows were drawn on the black line that pointed south. The black line went straight to Bellinger Airport, turned south and went straight through the Adirondacks. The only form of transportation that could follow this route was an airplane. Why would the driver need to know an airplane route if he was driving a stolen Jeep?

A red X was drawn on the map in nearly the same location that he was sitting. Another mark on the map was made on the ridge that Jack had pointed to moments ago. There was nothing on that ridge except a nice view. It seemed to be almost a mile from the parked Jeep and would have been a steep, arduous climb through thick briar patches and dense woods. Hiking up the hill without snowshoes would be an exhausting journey.

"What the hell?" Eric asked himself. His thoughts were interrupted by the blue Dodge pulling up next to him.

"Well," Jack chided from the passenger seat, "You coming, or did your ass freeze to the seat?"

"I think we better report this," Eric said. "If this Jeep is stolen..."

Jack interrupted, "Already tried," holding up his cell phone. "No service up here, remember?"

Eric checked his own phone to be sure. Same. He folded the map and brought it with him. If nothing else, it would give them something to look at today if the fishing was slow. He climbed in the back seat of Paul's truck, and they pulled away. They had four more miles to reach their destination and a quarter-mile walk from there. If the Jeep were still there when they came back through that night, they would report it once they returned to town. For now, it wasn't going anywhere, and the fish were getting ready to bite.

Paul shifted the truck into four-wheel-drive and eased away. Eric unfolded the map in the back seat and took another look.

"What's that?" Paul asked, looking in the rearview mirror.

"A map of New York."

"Jesus, Eric, we know where we're going," Jack joked.

"It was in that Jeep. There's an X on the map right where the Jeep was parked. Another one on the ridge where the driver was headed."

"Probably a photographer trying to catch the sunrise over the mountains," Paul said.

"Why would a photographer steal a vehicle to do that?" Jack asked.

Paul realized his theory didn't make sense. "Why would anyone drive through a snowstorm in the middle of the night, to a place like this?"

They all tried to come up with an answer, but nothing seemed to make sense. The conversation finally turned back to fishing and the day ahead.

Chapter 4 / *Plan in Motion*

Stealing the Jeep was easy. The Canadian had driven Moonie's truck as far as he dared. He didn't risk stopping to refuel the black F-150—gas stations were covered in security cameras—so it was better to have acquired a new vehicle. He made it to northern Higley on fumes and found a busy little tavern to park. The parking lot was full of opportunity. He had parked in the darkest corner and hoped that one trusting fool had left their keys in the ignition. As he crept through the dark parking lot, he had found several vehicles unlocked, but none with keys. The music playing inside was loud and obnoxious, but it covered any sound he was making outside. A drunk couple on the front porch had never noticed the Canadian. The female was sitting on the deck railing with her legs locked around the young male. They neither saw nor cared about anything going on in the parking lot.

He didn't have to search for long. A green Jeep with a frog decal on the back window was unlocked, and the keys were located inside the center console. The Jeep was wearing a set of 32- inch Cooper tires with an aggressive mud and snow tread. The spare was mounted to the tailgate. The bright green paint had a few rust spots on the running boards, but that was normal this far north where the roads received salt during the winter months. Not the most inconspicuous vehicle, but the four-wheel drive would be handy traversing the hazardous roads. He would have an hour headstart before the bar closed, and the Jeep would be reported as stolen. That hour would give him time to reach his destination and abandon the stolen Jeep.

He laid his pistol on the passenger seat in case his grand larceny was noticed and fired up the beastly 4x4. The cold engine fired immediately and softly purred as six cylinders compressed air and fuel. The Canadian smiled in satisfaction. He had worried that the tough looking jeep would roar when he engaged the ignition, drawing attention to himself from the rightful owner.

Route 56 would lead him south most of the way. The green Jeep made its way down the road as it meandered through the foothills and along the Raquette River. He turned left when he finally arrived at the most southern bridge, crossing to the eastern side of the river, and drove one more mile. At 1:30 am, he had reached an access road that led to a couple of hydroelectric power facilities. The sign at the beginning of the road indicated it was Garrison Road and, according to the map, it followed the river south for nine miles until it dead-ended at a hunting club. He parked the Jeep in the middle of the one-lane gravel road, knowing no plow trucks would be cleaning this road today. It was New Year's Day, and most of the highwaymen were spending the holiday at home. Snow maintenance on Garrison Road was probably the responsibility of the power company, anyway. Hunters were not a concern, either, since the season on whitetail deer had ended a month ago.

He stepped outside and stood still for a moment. The silence in this part of the world was almost frightening. He could not remember ever being in a place so void of even the faintest sound. His footsteps crunched on the dry ground and disrupted the forest's tranquility, and the Canadian felt rude for doing so.

Again, he closed his eyes, and the vision of the tombstone replayed in his mind.

This time, it was covered with snow, and two doves were perched on top. He reached out to brush the snow from the letters engraved in the marble, scattering the two doves and sending them frantically into flight. Their wings whirled the snow from atop the stone as the wind blew it into his face. The cold of the snow shocked him back to reality, and he was happy to see he was not standing in a cemetery, but still in the woods of northern New York. With a deep breath, he pushed the vision of the tombstone out of his mind and concentrated on his mission.

The backpack was heavy, but once strapped properly on his shoulders, was of little encumbrance. His determination to get to the top of the ridge far outweighed the loaded pack. He double checked his pockets and ensured all the zippers were secured, then took one last look in the vehicle to be sure he left nothing behind. The map still lay on the back seat, but that was of no further use to him since it had already served its purpose by getting him there.

It was easier to hike the darkness without the aid of a flashlight. Every time he tried to turn on his headlight, it illuminated only the trees immediately in front, blinding him to whatever lay beyond them. The short depth of view was of no use to him and disrupted his sense of direction.

"Better to just use the moonlight," he thought.

The snow on the ground silhouetted the trees like a painting he'd once seen in a museum. The Adirondack forest lit only by the moon was surely a masterpiece that could not be forgotten.

The snowstorm had pushed by, once again revealing the moon pitched high in the sky. It was surrounded by tiny stars that stayed in place as if it had an army of minions. The next storm was predicted to invade the area around 8:00 a.m. The army of stars would retreat by then, and the sun would take over as ruler of the sky. That would give him almost six hours to trek up the ridge, get some food, and hopefully a quick nap.

He saw the ridge in silhouette and singled out a pointed knob. That would be his destination. He had made his way through beech whips, alders, and briar patches, which were dense and hard to traverse. It was a frustrating climb as the backpack snagged several times, slowing his ascent and throwing off his balance. Once he was through the dense vegetation of the lower altitude, the deciduous forest opened up and was easier to navigate. He had weaved his way through mature ash, poplar, black cherries, and beech trees. His optimism had risen like the hilly terrain he was determined to conquer.

The snow was dry and light which made it easier to stride as the middle-aged man climbed the steep hill. Though the distance was short, he placed his steps carefully and took ample time to march the incline. The snow-covered logs, rocks, and holes were hazardous, and each step had to be placed with caution. Perspiration began to form on his skin which was sticky and uncomfortable. He uzipped his jacket in an attempt to cool his body. Sweating could lead to hypothermia once he stopped which would hinder his motor skills and ability to make a significant fire.

The climb had been much more arduous than he had anticipated. Three-quarters of the way up, he came to a rock face that was impossible to scale without the proper gear. He stared at the 15-foot granite impasse discouragingly. "Damn it!"

The bedrock that stood before him was about 180 feet long and tapered back into the earth on both ends. He studied the wall of stone for a few minutes, looking for his best option. It was to the north. The rock wall ran along the upper half of the ridge before diving back into the soil like a train descending into an underground tunnel. Walking along the cliff until he could turn and start to climb again would expend precious calories and energy. His leg muscles burned from the build-up of lactic acid and he wanted to rest. He wanted to drop the backpack and sit down, but he knew that was a luxury he did not have.

The tombstone flashed in his mind.

"No," he whispered. "I will not rest."

His nostrils flared as he sucked in as much oxygen as he could, then expelled the used air from his lungs. He grabbed the straps of the backpack and sinched them tighter, pulling the weight of the pack high on his back.

"Forward and upward," he said. The small trees along the cliff were great for balance. He gripped them one-by-one and made his way along the rock.

The detour around the cliff was more dangerous and exhausting than he had foreseen. He had fallen twice, breaking his attitude but not his determination. His face flushed with exertion and frustration as he traversed the rugged hillside. Perseverance was his only option at this point. The top of the ridge was so close, yet seemed so far to his tired legs. Rounding the corner of the cliff and seeing open woods brought a smile to his face. There were no more obstacles to impede his path, and his satisfaction rose like the few thin maples that surrounded him.

When he had reached the top of the ridge, he freed his shoulders from the weight of the heavy backpack and fell to his knees. His break was brief, and he began to build a small fire. He cleared snow from the ground, built the small but sufficient fire, and set a couple of logs up as a makeshift bench. He unzipped a side pocket of the backpack and retrieved a can of soup, a protein bar, and a canteen.

The fire heated the can of soup, and once it reached a suitable temperature, he dug in with a spoon and savored the nourishment. He had not eaten in 14 hours, and if everything went according to plan, he would be too busy to eat again until later in the evening.

He finished eating and packed his garbage into a plastic bag. There was no sense in leaving anything behind. If he could carry it in full, he could carry it out empty. Besides, he could not take the chance his garbage would become evidence. The coals in the fire had lost most of their heat, so the Canadian added a small pile of beech wood branches that burned hot and slow. Just what he needed right now. Once the fire had rekindled, he leaned against a large black cherry tree and closed his eyes. This time, he would not envision the solemn grave with its marble headstone. He would drift off into a light sleep and wait for his phone alarm to go off in about an hour.

****

Before sleep overtook him, the Canadian replayed the last three weeks of his life in his mind. He thought about how this plan came to fruition and how fate had brought him to the top of this ridge. He thought about the airport, the pilot, the airplane, and the money.

He worked as an aircraft mechanic at a small airport outside of Ottawa, although he spent most of his time working on everything but planes. The airport was for private charters. Carl Skiff, the owner of Red-Wing Charters, made his living with a couple of Beechcraft Bonanza A-36's. Most of the charters carried small loads of cargo. Skiff had the seats removed from one of his planes to accommodate the extra space needed for shipping items in bulk. The second plane had only two passenger seats, but the other four could easily be reinstalled for extra passengers. Most of the cargo was comprised of merchandise stuffed with drugs. The opiate market was booming in New York and Canadian cities, and Red-Wing Charters was delivering a percentage of the drugs. Planes rarely came back empty after making deliveries, because the return flights often carried guns, illegal aliens, or black-market merchandise; all of which was usually shipped out again. The little airport was a turnstile of illegal activity.

Before he'd crossed the border and put a bullet into Moonie Swamp, the Canadian lived a normal life, worked 40 hours per week, and was a model citizen in his neighborhood. He'd had some trouble with the law in his younger years, which prevented him from being legally able to enter the United States. Of course, he had no reason to enter New York State until he heard a phone conversation Skiff was having with an associate.

 The mechanic was working on the airport's heating system when the conversation carried through the air ducts.

"Three point five?" Skiff barked. "Are you frickin crazy, Polina? Okay…Okay, but I'm only sending three

47

million...American currency....No, one case...Shit...Okay...We'll leave here on the first...No, January first...That's right...Wheels leave the ground at 6:50 in the morning...Of course, we'll fly to you. Have a driver ready and waiting. Blankenship—you remember Mason—he'll personally be carrying the money...Yes, he's still single, Polina. Do I get a discount if he'll take you out for dinner? Ha ha...He'll have the money. No, the border's no problem. I've got connections in New York."

So, the flight was to depart on New Year's Day, at 6:50 a.m. He knew the time of departure but not the destination or arrival time. The Beechcraft A-36 Bonanza would be carrying nothing but a briefcase with three million dollars. The case would be locked up and guarded in Ottawa by Skiff's goon, Mason Blankenship, who'd be armed with his HK-416 A5 assault rifle. Mason would accompany the case until they reached their destination. Stealing the money in Ottawa was a suicide mission. Stealing the money wherever the plane landed might be impossible. The only plan that would work—steal the money somewhere in the middle. It seemed dangerous. It seemed impossible. How do you rob a plane that's flying fifteen hundred feet above the ground when you're not on board?

The solution hit him like a bug on a windshield. It would be a challenge, but he was confident he could pull off the heist if he could acquire the plane's destination within the next few days.

****

The Canadian had seen guns, drugs, and foreigners loaded onto the planes but never any money. He'd kept his mouth shut for years without getting anything larger than a $500 bonus—which he thought was good money until he heard about the $3 million.

He needed more details about the flight to pull off such a heist and the best place to get the intel was from the pilot scheduled to fly the Beechcraft. There was only one place to find pilots near the airport—the Bombardier Lounge—an overpriced gentleman's club run by a retired airman. It was the preferred watering hole for pilots to hang out during long layovers or canceled flights. All the Canadian had to do was buy a few rounds of Labatt Blues at the Bombardier, and the local pilots were verbal sprinklers—spouting and bragging about their missions in every direction. The inebriated pilots would talk about private charters, airforce missions, and mistresses—most of which was probably not true.

It was a Tuesday night when the Canadian finally discovered who the unfortunate pilot would be. He was a resident pilot that everyone called Ozzy. He was a thin man, not weighing more than 150 pounds. The Canadian often wondered how the little man could control a turbulent plane with such scrawny arms. He knew Ozzy from the airport but heard he had relocated to Alaska to become a bush pilot. His employment there only lasted a month. Ozzy was fired when he took a small group of children on a field trip to Anchorage, and a bottle of blackberry schnapps rolled out from under the seat. The teacher might have overlooked the incident, but a couple of parents

49

chaperoning the trip filed a formal complaint immediately upon landing, and now he was back at the Bombardier Lounge, drinking with his brotherhood of pilots and taking any contract Skiff would offer him.

The Canadian wished it were another pilot. As much of a screw-up as Ozzy was, he was a good guy. But on the bright side, Ozzy had a mouth as loose as a hula hoop, and getting him to drop the details on the Beechcraft flight would be as easy as getting a goat to eat.

****

The Canadian and Ozzy played pool while a couple of girls working their way through college danced with a stainless steel pole. They winked at the Canadian as he walked by carrying his third round of draft beers. He smirked a little but resisted the urge to sit and watch the dancers work. His resistance pissed the girls off, and the wink flipped to a scowl.

The Bombardier Lounge was located on a side street in Ottawa's Industrial Park. The building sat adjacent to a vacant lot and only a couple blocks from the train yard. There was a certain irony that an aviation-themed bar thrived so close to the train yard. The pilots often made jokes about train engineers having too much lead in their ass to get off the ground, or how they were too stupid to find their way home without tracks. The mechanic wasn't a fan of the off-colored humor. He respected the train engineers and what they accomplished, and he marveled at the engines of the train and the power they produced.

The small warehouse, about the size of a high school gym, had been gutted and remodeled twice in the last 30 years. Rustic pine boards paneled the walls three feet high around the interior of the lounge. Maps, airplane models, and vintage aviation photos decorated the walls. They were enhanced with spotlighting and LED signs that gave an incandescent glow to the whole place. The center of the lounge was occupied by two small stages for dancing, with a D.J. booth keeping a watchful eye over both.

The masterpiece of the Bombardier Lounge was the bar itself. It was 24 feet long and shaped like an airplane wing. The top was polished aluminum panels that were riveted together just like the skin of old B-2 bomber. Bullet holes, scratches, and burn marks were added for effect.

The pool table was hidden in the back corner behind a partition, where players could watch the dancers while they played. The Canadian liked playing pool in the corner, which was a great area to escape the stench of stale beer.

Ozzy was waiting for his beverage at the pool table, watching the girls from afar. He held a cue stick vertically in front of himself, mimicking the girls on the poles—his hips and shoulders swayed in perfect time to a Theory of a Deadman song blasting over the speakers. He only stopped so he could grasp the stein of beer the Canadian was carrying in his left hand.

"Thanks, lad," Ozzy mumbled. He gulped down a quarter of the mug's contents, set the beer on a high-top, and then studied the scattered billiards on the green felt. Ozzy lined up for a shot while the Canadian continued his interrogation.

"What's your schedule look like for the next couple of weeks, Oz?" the Canadian asked the pilot.

"Nine-ball in the side pocket," the pilot said. He ignored the stocky mechanic to focus on a bank shot. The nine-ball dropped in the intended pocket, and Ozzy chalked up his cue stick for the next shot.

"Skiff has me doing a ton of work on the Beechcraft. Making sure it's in top-notch condition," the Canadian said. "She's in good shape to make it to Sudbury if that's where you're headed." The Canadian knew all-to-well, that was not where the plane would land. He took a swig of lager, waiting for the pilot to correct him.

"Sudbury? I ain't going to no frickin Sudbury. Five-ball, corner pocket."

"Oh, sorry, I just assumed…"

"No, fuck that place, eh?" The five-ball dropped in the corner pocket. "I hope I never go back to Sudbury. Last time I was in that shit-hole, a goddamn fisherman nearly shot my ear off. Course, I was out in his boat, with his wife, so can't say as I blame the guy."

The Canadian chuckled at the story.

"No, I'm headed down to Schenectady," Ozzy finally revealed.

"The States? New York, eh?" The Canadian's face twisted at the thought of the plane leaving the country. On the other hand, getting away with the money would be easier if he was in another country. Factor in that he was going to head south with it anyway, and it might actually make his plan easier to pull off.

"Seven in the corner."

The seven dropped in the intended pocket.

"Aye, I've got to go to New York, then I'm leaving there for Burlington," Ozzy's Irish accent always came out when he talked about flying. Usually, it was in the company of pretty women. The prettier the woman, the heavier the accent became.

New York was going to be a problem. With his criminal background—a DWI and some charges for an unlicensed weapon—getting into New York would be impossible— legally, anyway. He needed to find someone to get him across the border, and he needed to do it soon.

"You sure about that, Oz?"

"Sure, I'm sure. Just like I'm sure I'm kicking your ass in this game, lad." Ozzy chalked the cue stick again. "Three in the corner, off the eleven." He drew the cue stick back, carefully aiming at the three-ball. He imagined the ball ricocheting off the eleven and into the corner. When he was happy with the angle, he drew back the cue stick and then launched it at the intended target. Like a firing pin of a rifle, it struck the three-ball and knocked it across the green table. The three-ball bounced off the eleven, just like he'd planned, and into the corner pocket. The eleven-ball was knocked across the table, and struck the black eight-ball. The momentum from the eleven set the eight-ball into motion and Ozzy watched with disgust as the eight-ball fell into the opposite corner pocket.

"Aww, bloody hell!" Ozzy protested as the black ball dropped into the angular pocket. "Didn't see that coming."

"No, you didn't. You never know what's coming, Oz'," the Canadian smiled in victory. "Sorry ol' buddy, you lose."

****

After dumping Ozzy in an Uber and paying the driver himself, the Canadian went home and fired up his laptop. He searched the plane's path on Skyvector, an application that tracks flights and maps flight paths. Skyvector showed the plane's path from Ottawa to Schenectady went directly through the Adirondack Mountains in New York.

The Canadian couldn't believe his luck. The flight path passed over the perfect place for him to complete the heist.

Chapter 5 / *Bear Bay*

Paul Marten pulled a large plastic sled down the river bank and onto the ice. The hike from the truck was a quarter of a mile, and he and his brothers were making good time. The trail had a solid base from a group of snowmobiles that had traveled through here weeks before, and only a couple of snowdrifts slowed their hike. He looked at the contents of the sled to ensure nothing had fallen out or spilled. When he was sure his gear was still secured, he continued across the frozen river bay. Jack and Eric weaved through the pines, following Paul's tracks. Their pace quickened when they reached the open ice.

They crossed Bear Bay and parked their sleds on the south shore. There was a strategy to their location. The tall pines would protect them from the west wind if it began to blow and they could keep their backs to the sun most of the day as they watched their tip-ups—although, there wouldn't be much sun today. The sun's rays reflecting off the snow were harsh on an ice fishermen's eyes and capable of burning the retina. The Martens needed to be cautious of developing snow-blindness, so they wore sunglasses and faced north.

After deciding where to set up their tip-ups, they started to work. Jack pushed the rubber bulb on his ice auger, forcing fuel into the carburetor, and primed the engine. He set the choke, pulled the start cord 4 times and the 52 cc engine sputtered. He opened the choke back up and tried again. The little engine came to life, spewing exhaust fumes as the sound of the two-stroke engine disrupted the silence of the forest. Jack pushed the throttle gently with his thumb to allow the engine time to warm up. Cold oil inside the crankcase was heating up, losing viscosity, and lubricating the interior engine parts. Jack was too impatient to wait any longer—it was time to drill holes and get fishing.

He swept his boot from side to side, revealing the hard ice that supported him. The auger growled, and the eight-inch-wide drill spun faster. The aggressive blades chewed a hole through the ice in seconds. When the auger finished boring through the hard ice, Jack eased off the throttle and lifted it out of the hole, pulling a gush of water with it that flooded the ice. The gush of water was intentional. Jack knew it would freeze the snow in a four-foot radius around the hole and prevent the wind from blowing snow into the hole and covering up the tip-ups.

"Fourteen more to go," Jack thought. He paced off 15 yards to drill the next hole. He would continue drilling until he had three rows of five holes—one row for each fisherman.

Paul carried a sweetgrass pack basket containing six wooden tip-ups. Although he could only use five by law, it was always a good idea to have a spare. He knelt at the first hole and unfolded the wooden tip-up. The base swiveled to resemble an inverted cross; then he loosened a wing-nut which allowed another wood piece to swivel and form an X for a stable base. The spool on the side of the tip-up held a 25-pound test fishing line, braided for extra strength and flexibility. An Octopus hook adorned the business end of the line, which allowed for easier removal and less harm to the fish.

Paul peered into the dark water, wondering about the depth. The lead weight clipped to his jacket—a depth finder—would give him the answer. He attached the orange depth finder to the hook. The lead weight was molded around a large alligator clip to bite and hold the hook. Once secure, he lowered the combination into the river water and let it sink until it reached the bottom. His thumb and index finger pinched the fishing line at the top of the water, and then he pulled the rest of the line up by hand and let it coil neatly on the ice. He looked at the unspooled line and ascertained that the river was about 12-feet deep in this area.

"Twelve feet!" Paul shouted to Eric. Eric responded with a thumb pointing upward.

Paul removed the depth finder from the hook and replaced it with a three-inch long minnow. He forced the hook through the minnow's back, just behind the dorsal fin, careful not to hit the spine, and dropped it into the water. The minnow was shocked from the cold water at first, but once his body temperature adjusted he sank toward the river bottom. Paul wound a few feet of line back onto the spool to ensure his bait would not loiter at the bottom of the river.

"Now, we're fishing," Paul thought to himself. He moved hurriedly from hole to hole, repeating the process and completed his set in about 12 minutes. Eric had set one of Jack's tip-ups at each of the first five holes and was working on his own when Paul finished. Paul hauled his gear back to the shoreline and cleared an area to start a fire. The three brothers worked fast and efficiently, leaving little time to converse until they were set up for the day. By the time Jack had finished drilling holes and setting up his tip-ups, Paul's fire was glowing with life under the thick pine trees. The smell of burning pine drifted with the gentle west wind.

They didn't need the fire for warmth. The temperature was just a few degrees below freezing. The fire was like having another soul fishing with them—a soul that was warm and energetic. Its constant dance was entertaining, and its energy was contagious. They watched the fire while waiting for a fish to trigger the flags on their tip-ups. Gathering wood was something to keep them occupied, and eventually, they would need it to cook their lunch.

The brothers convened at the fire, poking the ashes and retelling stories of their past fishing trips. Jack lit a cigarette and sat in a nylon chair he had brought with him. He looked at Eric and smirked, "Hey Eric, remember to stay away from the brook today."

Eric peered to the southwest corner of the bay. It was an area that rarely froze over because of the rushing water from a large brook that merged with the river. Any ice that did form was too thin to hold the weight of a man. Eric recalled his experience two years prior when the brothers were fishing this bay for the first time.

It was colder than they had expected that day, and the 20-miles-per-hour wind blew steady. Even so, they decided to stay and fish until after lunch.

Eric was pulling dead branches from a hemlock tree when he noticed something sticking out of the ice about 30 yards from the shore. He walked out onto the ice about 10 yards to get a better look. He recognized the shape but was baffled by its presence. Marching through eight inches of snow, he made his way out until he was close enough to reach down and grab the antler of a white-tailed deer. The antler was frozen in the ice, but he gave it a little tug. It would not budge. He thought about fetching his ice spud to chip away the ice, but the snow was deep, and his legs were already tired from exerting himself all morning. He pulled harder, trying to force the antler to break free of the ice's frozen grip.

The force of his pull put increased weight on his feet—a weight that the thin ice was not capable of supporting. Eric crashed through the ice without warning. He felt the icy water flood his clothes and leech into his boots. A flurry of bubbles rose around him, disorienting his sense of direction. Half of his breath was forced out of his lungs as the cold water shocked his body. Now, nearly out of oxygen and stuck in waterlogged boots, he began to sink to the bottom of the Raquette River. That was not something he had expected to happen that day. That was not how he thought he would die, but there was little he could do. His body had no buoyancy, and he would go unconscious in minutes. Had Jack and Paul seen him go through the ice? He looked up at the jagged opening he had created. He could not see his older brothers—brothers who had protected him his whole life from neighborhood bullies, vicious dogs, and dangerous situations. Brothers who helped him learn sports, finish his homework, finish his chores, and took the blame when he shot Mr. Graham's car with a BB gun. Where were they now? Where were they when he needed them most?

Eric gave up looking for his brothers and was nearly ready to give up on his life. He felt something bump on his back and spun in the water to see what was there. Even though he had only sunk about seven feet, it was dark this deep down. Still, he could see the silhouette of a deer against the ice above. The deer was still attached to the prize antler that had caused this situation. His numb fingers reluctantly grasped the deer's hind leg. Eric's arms were weak and tired of trying to fight the current. He pulled himself upward and grabbed the deer's front leg, then reached further to grasp the one antler that was below the surface of the ice. Now his head was almost to the top, but his body wanted to drift back to the bottom. Blackness began to creep into his vision, and it seemed as though he was peering into a tunnel. He closed his eyes tight, not wanting to watch the blackness take him.

"Perhaps," he thought, "It would be easier to just stop fighting. Let the blackness take over and end this."

He opened his eyes. He was staring eye-to-eye with the deceased deer. This magnificent animal, once strong and exuberant, had been taken by the ice, and Eric decided they would not share the same fate. The deer's death reminded Eric how precious life was, and worth fighting for. Adrenaline surged through his veins as he pulled his feet up and hooked them into the deer's hind-quarters. It gave him enough of a boost that Eric could stick his face out of the water. He sucked in the wonderful oxygen which forced the darkness to retreat. He was too busy trying to catch his breath to yell for help. But the cold was working on his muscles and nerves. He wanted to pull himself out of the water, but his body would not cooperate. Something broke—but Eric wasn't sure what it was. More ice maybe? Whatever it was, it had been supporting his weight. The river began to pull again and would soon have its second victim. He saw the buck's eye again, which seemed to look at him with empathy. Eric closed his eyes and waited for the inevitable until he felt a tug on the back of his jacket.

Paul's long arm grasped his brother's coat with a grip like a pit bull's jaw. Every muscle in Paul's body pulled. Jack held onto both of Paul's boots to anchor him in place while he retrieved his little brother.

The river finally relinquished the youngest Marten brother from its icy bowels. They stayed on their bellies to distribute their weight and prevent a repeat of the event. Jack pulled Paul, Paul pulled Eric, and Eric pushed himself along. It wasn't until they were 10 yards from shore that they felt safe and could stop. Eric climbed to his knees and realized he was holding one of the deer's antlers in his right hand. He smiled in victory, elated to be alive.

Jack looked at Paul and back at their young brother. He was gasping for breath from the exertion and the fright of the situation. "Well, let's get you to the fire to warm up." He pointed at the antler, "Or, did you wanna go back and get the other one?"

The trio burst into laughter, and they never went near the brook again.

When they finished reminiscing about Eric's near-death experience, their attention turned back toward the tip-ups spread across the bay. The weather was so much nicer today than the day Eric almost drowned. They scanned their tip-ups, looking for any flags that might have been triggered by a fish during their reminiscing.

"Flag!" Paul yelled. "Jack, it's one of yours."

They jumped to their feet and jogged across the ice. The clunking of their heavy winter boots was as loud as their smiles were big. The clunking went on for 70 yards as they made their way to the hole. Jack slid to his knees just inches away from the hole. His breathing was heavy, and sweat was now beading on his forehead. The 70-yard jog had warmed him even more than the fire. His bare hand reached into the icy water to scoop out the slush forming at the top of the water. He gave his hand a shake to expel the cold water from his skin. Now, he had a clear view of the tip-up's spool. The submerged spool was spinning slowly as a northern pike swam away with the bait.

"Fish on," Jack whispered when he saw the moving spool. "I'll let him take a little more line. Let him swallow it." The line began to slow—a sure sign the pike was swallowing the bait and planning his next move. Once he decided, the spool spun wildly as the pike raced away.

"Now!" all three exclaimed in unison.

Jack pulled the tip-up out of the hole gently with his left hand. His right hand let the line glide through his thumb and index finger. Jacks hand clamped onto the runaway line, and in the same motion pulled backward, setting the treble hook deep into the pike's hard palate. The eldest Marten reeled in the line hand-over-hand, as the slack coiled in a pile on the ice. At first, the pike pulled and yarned on the line, trying to break free. Jack could feel the weight of the freshwater bruiser fighting back like a wild dog on a leash. Jack skillfully let the fish have his way on occasion, allowing the fish to flee with the taut line and the hook embedded in his jaw. The harder the pike pulled, the more exhausted he became—then it was Jack's turn. He pulled back again, spinning the fish 180 degrees and bringing him closer to the hole. It was back and forth this way for several minutes until finally, the fishes gills could not replenish the spent oxygen within his body, and he gave in to the human commanding the line.

A large eye came to the eight-inch hole drilled in the ice. Jack reached down with a gaff-hook and aligned the fish with the exit. Jack gently guided the gaff-hook through the opening in the fish's bottom jaw. The gaff-hook lifted like a crane, pulling the cold-blooded animal out of the water completely and laid it on the ice. From nose to tail, it measured 42 inches.

"Yahoo," Eric shouted. "Damn. She must be 12 pounds."

"Pretty close," Jack said as he carefully worked the Octopus hook out of the toothy mouth. When he finished, he reached into his pocket and pulled out his phone. Paul took the phone and snapped a couple of quick pictures.

"Keepin' him?" Eric asked.

"Nope. She's a good a breeder," Jack answered. "Too big to eat. Let's try to get some around twenty-four inches." He held the fish under the head, careful to avoid touching its gills. His other hand clenched the tail and gently guided the trophy fish home. "Go on girl," Jack encouraged her. With a couple of slow kicks, the pike swam away looking for a place to rest and regain its strength.

Paul waited for Jack to rinse his hands in the water and pat them dry on his overalls before handing back his phone. Jack re-spooled the fishing line, attached his depth finder and dropped it into the water. He then pulled the line back up and rebaited the hook with a minnow from the bucket Eric was carrying. A small flag, the size of a business card and mounted to a 20-inch long piece of thin steel, was bent downward and locked into place. When a fish took the bait, the spool would spin. The spinning spool would release the flag and allow it to spring upward. The bright orange flag, in contrast to the snow, could be seen from 100 yards away.

Paul was happy for Jack. Now, he wanted it to be his fight against the elusive northern pikes of the Raquette River. He scanned his tip-ups—his eyes darting from one and then the next, hoping to see one of the bright orange flags waving at him. When he focused on the furthest one, something else caught his attention—movement in the woods. He assumed it was a deer, browsing through the evergreens, but then realized that the shadow was coming toward them, and it was on two legs.

"Looks like we're not going to be alone today," Paul nodded toward the woods. He didn't want to stare at the man tentatively approaching—something about it seemed rude. He dropped his head and looked back at the tip-up that Jack was resetting. Blood from the thrashing fish had pooled adjacent to the hole. Diluted by the snow, the blood turned pink and spread across the ice in an area the size of a platter and Paul was standing right in it.

Chapter 6 / *The Inspection*

Ozzy was behind the control wheel of the Beechcraft A-36 flying south from Canada to New York. His only companion, Mason Blankenship, did not speak a single word all morning. The two occupants of the plane were both armed. Ozzy's side holster carried a .38 Special Taurus revolver. The sidearm was nothing fancy and came straight out of the box with no customization. Blankenship sat in the middle of the plane trying to doze off. His HK-416 leaned against the seat next to him. Foster sunglasses shaded his eyes, and he slunk down with his arms folded across his chest. It was difficult for the tall man to get comfortable within the confines of the aircraft. As cramped as he was, he was glad he was not sitting in the pilot's seat with all the flight controls, switches, and the yoke that cramped the cockpit. Blankenship often joked about planes being built by the Keebler Elves. Ozzy, with his small frame and thin arms, seemed to have plenty of space and looked comfortable at the controls. Luckily for Blankenship, the entire flight was only going to take about 82 minutes.

The first leg of the flight was from Ottawa to Bettinger Airport. International law required the Beechcraft to land at Bettinger for inspection. Once they touched down, the plane, pilot's license, passports, and all documents would be inspected. Ozzy wasn't worried about the inspection at Bettinger Airport because he knew the crooked Customs and Border Protection agent, Kyle Greene, would be performing the inspection. Carl Skiff had been paying off Greene for eight years, allowing his planes in and out of the U.S. without a thorough inspection or any hassle. The pilots just needed to tolerate Greene's cocky attitude and the verbal thrashings he liked to dish out.

Ozzy reduced the throttle, and the single-engine plane began to descend as it crossed over the St. Lawrence River, which divided the two countries. The river was a major shipping channel for both countries, and its surface was solid ice this time of the year, which forced the shipping season to be closed for the year. In the distance, Ozzy could see several state trooper cars racing up the highway toward the Saint-Regis Mohawk Reservation, their crimson lights flashing at high speed on the unusually desolate highway that ran parrelel to the river. Being a Saturday and a holiday, the lack of traffic made it easy for the police cars to zoom out of sight. Ozzy turned his attention back to his flight controls. He assumed there was probably an accident since the snow still plugged most of the secondary roads. He would never know the truth—that the police were called to the reservation to investigate the murder of a young Native-American male who was last seen smuggling a Canadian across the border.

Ozzy radioed the air traffic controller for the airport, which was in Burlington, Vermont. Bettinger International was too small to have an air traffic controller of their own, so all air traffic was controlled from a city 80 miles to the southeast.

"Burlington tower, Beechcraft Charlie Frank Bill Zebra Adam, one eight zero north inbound for landing with Bettinger," Ozzie spoke into his headset.

"Roger that, Beechcraft. You have permission and are clear for landing. Please proceed at two five zero, runway one left," an anonymous voice replied.

"Roger, Burlington tower. Beechcraft Charlie Frank Bill Zebra Adam proceeding to runway one left."

The wheels hit the tarmac of Bettinger International Airport at 7:25 am. Not their final destination, Bettinger was a small airport with only three outgoing flights per day that would accommodate nine passengers per flight if fully booked. And the planes only flew to three destinations—Boston, Syracuse, and Albany.

Ozzy brought the Beechcraft A-36 to a stop 200 yards from the terminal. The inspection would take place near the hanger. Ozzy wished they could have just flown straight to their destination, but all planes were required to stop for inspection by Customs and Border Protection when crossing into the Unitied States. Since their flight plan had been submitted hours ago, two Customs agents were already waiting for them to land.

A white and blue SUV was parked inside the chain-link fence that kept the general public from accessing the hanger area. The headlights were on while the engine ran and the windshield wipers cleaned the falling snow that tried accumulating on the glass. Ozzy throttled down and killed the plane's engine and waited in the cockpit for the officers to approach.

Officer Kyle Greene sat behind the wheel of the Chevy Tahoe. His partner, Officer Dishaw, watched Ozzy land and bring the plane toward the hanger through a set of Nikon binoculars.

"This our guy?" Dishaw asked.

"This is our guy," Greene answered. He was chewing on a toothpick and thumbing through his phone. An officer with Customs and Border Protection for almost 20 years, Greene was calm and patient as he waited to go perform the inspection. Dishaw had 18 months under his belt with the government agency, and the two of them had been partners for almost as long. Dishaw had somehow earned Greene's trust, and the two were usually the only officers assigned to do flight inspections.

Greene stepped out of the Tahoe and slipped on a dark blue ball cap with an agency logo embroidered on the front. His pants and shirt matched the hat, but his winter jacket was black. The ballcap resting on his head was six and a half feet off the ground. If he were to step on a pair of scales, he'd barely get over 170, but the bulletproof vest, thick winter jacket, and belt that holstered his pistol and gear made him look like he was 230. He marched toward the plane, carrying a clipboard in one hand.

Dishaw was younger. He was tall and athletic but standing next to Greene made him appear of normal height. He wore the same uniform as Greene and stayed one step behind him as the two made their way to the parked plane. Greene motioned for Ozzy to step out of the plane.

"Jesus, Ozzy, what the hell are you doing flying a nice plane like this?" Greene teased as Ozzy exited the cockpit door on the right side of the plane.

Ozzy stood on the right wing pointing with this thumb. "This piece o' shit? Thought it was a good plane, but the fucking altimeter just shit out on me, and a windshield wiper is about to fall off."

"Oh, well then, you should fail your inspection and call Uber to get your ass home," Greene threatened rhetorically as he signed the inspection form. He was focused on the inspection form and paperwork on the metal clipboard. Greene filled out the form without looking at any documents other than Ozzy's pilot license—only because he needed to record the license number. When he finished initialing here and signing there, he swung the clipboard with a backhand motion into Dishaw's chest, who took the clipboard without giving it a glance.

"So, let's go see what's on the plane. You wait with Dishaw. Oh, by the way," Greene said, pointing the used toothpick at Ozzy and then to Dishaw, "Ozzy, this is officer Dishaw. Officer Dishaw, this is nobody,"

"Screw you, Greene...and the horse you blew to get this job," Ozzy said.

"Skiff's goon inside, Ozzy?" Greene asked. He was pointing with the toothpick at the silhouette in the window.

"Mason? Yeah, I think he's asleep, so don't surprise him, lad. He's got that HK loaded and an itchy trigger finger. And he hasn't had his morning donut yet."

Greene opened the cargo door, bent his 6'6" frame, and squeezed into the plane so he would be out of sight. He hated getting on planes with his height. Once inside, he couldn't stand up, so he squatted while resting his arm on a small table that folded down.

Mason Blankenship appeared to be sleeping in the rear-facing seat behind the copilot's chair. His dark Foster sunglasses hid his steely eyes, but a faint smile told Greene the security brute was fully awake.

"Good Morning, Mr. Blankenship," Greene said. He knew Blankenship loved to get respect from people. It made him feel like more than just a bodyguard and a hired gun. Since he was nearly as tall as Greene and far deadlier with weapons or his hands, Greene gave him all the respect he wanted.

"Morning, Mr. Greene," Blankenship returned the respect. Greene noticed a silver case in the seat adjacent to the lone passenger.

"Well, everything looks good on board," Greene observed. "I don't see any illegal immigrants, can't smell any drugs, and everybody has their passports. You do have your passport, don't you, Mr. Blankenship?"

Blankenship's chiseled smile stayed intact. He leaned over to the silver case, set four numbers on the tumbler, and unlocked it. The case was loaded with American currency—all one-hundred dollar bills. On top of the money sat a manilla envelope with a name hand-written in black marker: "Greene." Blankenship passed the envelope to Greene, "Yes, Sir. Right here."

Greene took the envelope, peeked inside at the contents and guessed it was about $6,000—exactly what he expected. "Looks like all your paperwork is in order, Mr. Blankenship. You enjoy the rest of your flight." With that, he stepped out through the cargo doors, holding his back in pain. He slapped Ozzy on the back, "Everything appears to be in order, Ozzy. You may continue your flight. Just wait for clearance from the terminal before you take off."

"Yeah...thanks, Lad," Ozzy replied. "Suppose you'll be heading to the casino for the rest of the day, huh?"

"I wish. I'm heading back to the reservation, alright, but not to play blackjack. We had a homicide out there last night. A young smuggler, Moonie Swamp, was shot bringing an illegal across the Ice Bridge. The guy must have turned on him. Stole his truck, too. Too bad, Moonie was a good kid. He's earned me quite a bit of extra cash over the last few years."

"Bloody hell, Greene, is there anybody around here not paying you off?" Ozzy asked.

"Yeah...your mother. She's free, asshole." Greene handed the envelope to Dishaw. Dishaw's eyes and smile widening simultaneously as he peeked inside. Greene continued talking to Ozzy, "Seriously, Ozzy, you should get that windshield wiper fixed. There's a storm plowing through Higley—south of here about 40 miles—and you'll be flying right through it."

Ozzy shook his head. "Ah, I'll be fine, lad. But when I get back to the airport, I'm going to have a little chat with the fucking mechanic. I can't wait to see him again."

Greene and Dishaw made their way back to the Tahoe as Ozzy climbed aboard the Beechcraft. Greene tossed his toothpick to the ground."Take two grand out for yourself, Dishaw. Keep your mouth shut and don't deposit the money in the bank. These opportunities don't come along very often."

Dishaw pulled the cash out and separated 20 one-hundred dollar bills. Then he stuffed the remainder back in the envelope and shoved his cut into his front pocket. They climbed back into their white and blue vehicle and started to drive to the crime scene on the reservation. They were quiet as they each thought about what they'd do with their little bonus. Taking a bribe to let the plane pass inspection and carry that much money across the border seemed so easy to Dishaw. He could get used to these bonuses, and the exchange took place hundreds of yards from the terminal, where no one could see them. Or so he thought.

Stacie Marten set down the Leupold binoculars. She sat in the break room on the second floor of the Bettinger Airport terminal eating a light breakfast like she did every day she worked. The binoculars were just one set of three in the building and were used to watch for incoming flights, but they were also to ensure no deer or coyotes were wandering onto the tarmac when flights were departing or arriving. Today they served another purpose— watching two Customs and Border Protection agents take a bribe during a flight inspection.

Stacie set down the powerful optics and finished writing the plane's serial number on her napkin, "C-FBZA." She recognized Greene and wrote his name under the serial number. She always disliked Greene. The second officer was a new face to her, but she could get that information with a quick phone call to the Customs' office.

Ensuring private flights were legal was not part of Stacie's job duties, but she knew something was amiss about the whole ordeal. Customs inspections typically lasted 30 minutes, and this one was complete in the time it took her to make toast. The envelope of cash "new guy" was fumbling through reinforced the notion that she had just witnessed a bribe in progress.

She waited for the Beechcraft's wheels to leave the ground, tucked the napkin in her pocket, and headed to her office. Halfway down the hall, she turned right into the ladies room and vomited— nerves or her first bout of morning sickness, she wasn't sure, but she needed to make some phone calls and report the mysterious transaction.

72

She thought about Paul, standing on the ice, pulling in fish and laughing with his brothers. She tried sending him a text message—*Hope you ur having fun-Luv you. XOXO.*

Unable to send message, the phone blinked back at her. She knew Paul was out of cell phone range, but it was worth a try.

She dialed a number on her cell, calling Daryl downstairs. "Hey Daryl, it's Stacie."

Daryl worked for the airline. He was the ticket agent, luggage handler, and the flight director. He worked harder than anyone else at the airport, but for half the wages. "Hi, Stacie, what's up?"

"Was that Ozzy Sullivan flying that plane that just left?"

"Sure was. I know, I thought he'd moved to Alaska, too."

"Oh...I hadn't heard that. No, I was wondering where that flight was going. Did you receive an EAPIS report on that flight?"

"Yes, it was emailed to me. If I remember correctly, their destination is Schenectady. No cargo on board. One passenger—a guy by the name of Sunkenship, or Battleship, or something like that. I can't quite recall."

"Can you get me that name when you get back inside?" Stacie asked. She could see Daryl outside leaning on a snow shovel, holding the wireless phone to his ear.

"Yes, of course," Daryl replied. "I'll have it to you in about 10 minutes. Let me finish shoveling the sidewalk."

73

"Thanks," she hung up. Something had to be on that flight. Greene would only need to be bribed if there were guns, drugs, or illegal persons on board. Maybe there were more people on board than reported. Or, maybe this Sunken/Battleship guy was crooked. Obviously, he was using an alias. The questions kept building in her mind. The more she thought about it, the more it vexed her. How much cash did that sonovabitch just put in his pocket? Guilt burned in her chest and rose up into her throat. She poured her morning orange juice into her mouth and swallowed it down hard, hoping the guilt would be flushed with it. Was she jealous of Greene getting that money? She wondered what was bothering her more—the fact that they dared to commit a felony within view of the terminal or the fact that Greene probably walked away with enough cash to solve all her and Paul's money problems. She decided the answer was both.

Chapter 7 / *Ice Breaker*

Paul Marten watched the interloper veer from the snow-packed trail and step clumsily through knee-high snow. Jack stood from his kneeling position now that his tip-up was rebaited and set to spring once a fish took the bait.

"Andy Kessler," Jack identified the shadow. He could recognize a person's walk and silhouette better than he could identify vehicle tracks on the snow-covered roads. He'd watched Andy walk across the ice for years and knew the man well.

With an ice-fishing sled in tow, Andy Kessler snaked through some trees and started down a steep bank on the edge of the frozen river. His first step down the bank was a mistake, causing his left foot to slide forward while his right foot stayed planted behind. The awkward split position produced an imbalance that sent his arms flailing. With nothing to grab onto to regain traction or balance, he fell on his ass and disappeared in a puff of white powder. The jet-sled, loaded with gear, sped down the bank behind him, ran over his head and spilled its contents.

The Marten brothers fought to keep their laughter hidden, burying their faces in their buckskin mittens to muffle the sound. The clumsy fisherman sat straight up, snow packed in every crevice of his heavy coveralls and Carhart jacket. A pinky finger dug snow out of this left ear as he cocked his head sideways. Once the ear was clear, he kneeled on the ice and searched through the snow to retrieve his spilled gear.

The three Martens started scuffing across the ice to help Andy recover his gear. Eric spun on his heels. "Flag! It's one of mine. You guys go help Andy." Eric picked up the pace and jogged out to attend to his fish trap. Paul and Jack marched in the opposite direction to offer salutations and assistance to Andy.

By the time they reached his location, the snow that had gotten into Andy's jacket was melting. The cold water ran down his neck and back, stinging his skin and shocking his body. Andy was stripping off his heavy coat and chasing the wet snow running down his back and into his boots when he realized Paul and Jack were standing there watching him. The look of frustration disappeared as cheek muscles pulled the corners of his mouth back. Andy recognized the brothers immediately.

"Hey, Jack, how the hell are ya?" Andy greeted the oldest Marten.

"Good, Andy. Why didn't you stay on the trail?" Jack asked. "Jesus, you could've broken a leg or something."

"Thought I could make my own trail...hehe," Andy said, laughing at himself. "Didn't think that bank would be so slippery." He scanned the ice, surveying the tip-ups already in place and thought about where to drill a hole to jig for perch.

"Andy, you know my brother, Paul, don't you?" Jacked asked the burly man. Paul stepped forward with an ungloved hand.

"Oh yeah...hehe, how you doing, Paul," Andy asked, grasping Paul's hand with a firm shake.

"Good...good, thanks. How's the fishing been this year, Andy?"

"Not bad…hehe, not bad. Caught a nice northern out here last week. Too big. I decided to throw it back, 'cause I like the smaller ones for eating," he rubbed his protruding belly at the thought of eating fish.

Andy Kessler was a man everyone in town knew. He lived in his cabin just off the river, not far from where they were now standing. He did not work a traditional job, but rather, was a survivalist. Andy lived off the resources of the land, and was a skilled hunter, fisherman, and gardener. Many people envied Andy's lifestyle and how simply the man lived. A few had even tried to replicate his life by building cabins on the east side of the river until the isolation from society drove them back to civilization. But, Andy enjoyed the solitude of the woods.

People in town would see Andy year-round, despite his isolation. He was a friendly man, early 50s, with no wife or children. Every week, he would drive his truck to town and gather some supplies. He would often park at the fire station and sell firewood, fresh berries, baskets he had weaved, or traps he had built. The townspeople kept him busy with odd jobs and praised his work ethic. If you could contact him, Andy would perform any construction, cleaning, or repair around the house. The quality of his work was professional, and he charged half of what most contractors would.

Paul was kneeling on the ground, searching for Andy's gear in the snow. He retrieved an ice-spud, an ice scoop, and a minnow net. A Cobra CXT, two-way radio, found its way into Paul's hand. Paul curled the cuff of his buckskin mitten, revealing the wool lining and used it to brush away the snow packed into the speaker of the walkie-talkie. The radio squawked, surprising Paul.

Andy reached for the radio. "Oh, that stupid thing…picks up signals from all around us. I just keep it off."

He took the walkie-talkie from Paul and turned off the power. He reorganized the gear in his Jet Sled and started for the center of the bay. Jack and Paul walked on Andy's flanks, talking about their day so far, but all of them had eyes on Eric, kneeling at a hole, pulling fishing line hand-over-hand. A large walleye soon followed the line and lay on the ice flapping in protest. Paul and Jack broke into a slow jog, racing toward their young brother and leaving Andy behind.

Andy peeled to the left and stopped 50 yards from the brook. He lifted his auger from the sled and began cranking the six-inch hand drill, boring through the ice. Using a hand auger rather than a gas-powered, alleviated the extra weight and expense of gas. Thick arms, from years of manual labor, cranked the drill clockwise for 30 seconds until the drill dropped through. A gush of river water flooded the ice, melting the snow around the six-inch hole. The auger was set back in the sled, and Andy retrieved a small folding chair made of aluminum and canvas. The first hole he drilled was his last for the day. A small fishing rod, about 24 inches in length, was baited with a small minnow. Andy intended to sit and catch a few perch for today and leave the bigger fish for another time. He jigged his rod in a slow upward motion then let the bait settle back down. The motion repeated over and over, and it wasn't long before a 10-inch perch showed interest.

Chapter 8 / *Cordelia*

The Canadian hiked in circles on top of the ridge for no other reason than to warm up. He collected firewood along the way, even though the use of the fire would soon come to an abrupt end. The sun was illuminating the hillside now. He peered down the cliff, staring at his tracks in the snow, meandering through the diversity of trees and climbing with determination. The ridge appeared so much smaller in the daylight. Was it because the darkness had concealed the scale of the granite ridge, tricking him into believing he had climbed higher than his current elevation? Or was it the snow that had fooled him, forcing his steps to be high as he picked up his boots with every step? He rubbed his legs, thinking about how they had burned from fatigue earlier that morning. He peeked at the cheap watch strapped to his wrist.

7:25

Time to get busy.

The backpack leaned against the cherry tree where he had slept. He pulled it closer to the fire and unzipped the top, exposing a black plastic case the size of a pillow. The case sat on the ground in an area of packed snow, not too far from the fire. Inside, the contents included two batteries, a remote control, an iPhone, a bag of spare parts, and a quadcopter that the Canadian had built himself. Flying remote aircraft became a hobby for the mechanic three years prior when he had observed a helicopter at the airport where he worked.

He envied the pilot behind the controls—rising, spinning in 360s, hovering over the city like a superhero waiting for the public's laudation. The aerial machine fascinated him. While most people only saw the big machine with a giant rotor, he thought about all the internal parts working in harmony—perfectly timed mechanisms; electricity being produced, torque converted to power, the power turning rotors, the rotors supplying lift. It was a thing of beauty, and the mechanic watched with the same awe that a luthier might watch a symphony. All those essential parts synchronized to play and work together in harmony to form a powerful masterpiece.

That very day, a new remote-controlled helicopter occupied the back seat of his Silverado. It wasn't long before he was adept at flying the toy aircraft and yearned for more power and speed. He perused online forums, bought books to study, and joined a local RC club. Within a year, he was ordering parts and building RC aircraft for racing. His favorite was a quadcopter he called Cordelia; named after a song by The Tragically Hip—not realizing the reference came from *King Lear*.

The diameter of the drone was about 30 inches once the arms unfolded. The Canadian inspected each rotor blade, the gas lines, and the wiring. The remote control batteries were at full charge. Good. The little gas engine, the heart of Cordelia, was from a Stihl 56 RC weed eater. The engine could produce one horsepower with its 27 cc engine, and fly for almost an hour.

He pushed the primer bulb five times and pull-started the engine. Cordelia coughed, but was reluctant to start in the cold. He switched the choke lever to the cold position and tried again, but to no avail. He cranked five more times. This time, the little engine whined at him and then idled down to a quiet rumble. The two-stroke engine idled until he pushed forward on the right stick of the remote.

Cordelia came to life and rose from her base. She hovered like a hungry bumble bee, ready to feed on a succulent flower. The Canadian watched the five-inch screen mounted on the remote control as he guided Cordelia higher. She climbed unobstructed over the treetops, her single lens staring downward, unblinking, shutter open, and aperture set.

"Sorry, Cordelia," the Canadian said. "Won't be any pictures today."

Cordelia turned her eye toward the horizon and then spun 360 degrees. A horde of clouds stormed into view to the north, obscuring visibility in a white haze. This was the direction from where the target would be approaching. The other 270 degrees were much more clear with a cyan sky washed with stratus clouds like freshly cleaned sheets hanging on a clothesline, blowing in the wind in slow motion.

Cordelia finished her test flight and descended to the ground.

Luckily, a large cherry tree had fallen here some time ago, uprooted by a wind storm. Several smaller trees lay under the large cherry tree as collateral damage to the violent fall. The missing trees created a void in the canopy of branches above. The void allowed the sunlight and rain to penetrate the forest and nurture new growth. It was the perfect example of how nature worked— old must die so new can be born, or in this case, grown. The old tree would rot away and fertilize the young saplings growing in the sun, nourishing their bark and leaves so they would be healthy and strong. The death of the large cherry was a melancholy event, but necessary. If the mature trees continued to live, they would suffocate the new flora, robbing it of a chance to grow and thrive.

That's how nature was supposed to work. Old dies so the young can survive.

The vision of the tombstone zipped through the Canadian's mind faster than Cordelia could fly a circle around him.

A deep breath of cold New York air filled his lungs to bursting capacity. He exhaled with force, clearing his lungs, his mind, and his conscience. Cordelia was parked on the packed snow in front of him, her all-seeing camera pointing straight out to where he was sitting. The Canadian walked over and hit the kill-switch to stop the engine, then returned to the log where he'd been sitting.

"Don't look at me like that."

Cordelia continued to stare.

"I know...I know, but Jesus, this is what I have to do. We've come this far, no sense turning back now, eh. Besides, ya know, this is my only shot. I fail today, there is no hope. No hope at all."

His eyelids swelled a little, fighting the urge to burst.

Cordelia sat unresponsive by his argument. Her four arms reached upward, lifted as though giving up on the Canadian and asking forgiveness from a higher power.

"You do your job, and I'll do mine. Everything will be okay."

A single tear fell from the human's eye and disappeared somewhere in his red beard. He stood abruptly, fighting the weakness that had momentarily overtaken his determination. Two hands clenched into fists, pulling the skin taught over thick bony knuckles. The fists finally relaxed and reached into the open backpack to retrieve a canister.

The canister was a galvanized steel cylinder about six inches in length with a diameter of two inches. One side had a steel cap threaded over the end. The steel cap was drilled out in the center, and the hole was threaded to accommodate a spark plug. Two wires ran from a battery to a remote switch and then to the spark plug. Once the switch was turned on, the set-up created an internal spark—a spark that would ignite four ounces of gunpowder. The rest of the canister space was full of ball bearings—the smallest were the size of BB's, the largest were similar to marbles. The opposite end of the canister was then sealed off by a thin piece of galvanized steel welded into place. The entire thing was, virtually, an oversized shotgun shell with an electric primer.

The canister mounted to Cordelia's back with the help of some pre-fastened velcro and a couple of zip-ties. The wires peeking through the end of the canister were attached to a whip that was ready to receive them. The Canadian had removed all of Cordelia's lights and rearranged the wires to act as the ignition for the homemade pipe bomb. Once he hit the light switch on the remote control, the spark plug would ignite the gunpowder. The explosion inside would be contained, blowing the ball bearings out of the weaker end of the canister.

The Canadian finished strapping the pipe bomb to loyal Cordelia and sat , staring at his device of destruction. He listened to the silence. The wind moved like a ninja through the leafless trees, leaving the snow and everything it touched undisturbed. The only evidence of its existence was the temperature change on the Canadian's face. A chickadee fluttered from branch to branch in a thin gray birch tree, scouring the dry catkins for seeds. Each time she changed location, she announced it with her delicate voice. The Canadian watched her movements hypnotically as she danced, fluttered, and sang. He felt as though this tiny bird might be trying to tell him something and he enjoyed her company. Then she was gone.

His attention turned back to the silence. Cordelia watched him stoically, waiting to serve him loyally and execute her orders without hesitation. Her controls rest in the Canadian's lap as he thumbed the joysticks and thought about her mission. With his eyes closed, he focused and listened for the sound of their intended target.

He didn't have to wait long.

In the distance, coming from the north, the sound came as a whisper on the wind. He heard the distinct sound of the engine he had worked on many times in the past. He heard the propeller chopping at the wind with its high-speed revolutions. The sound grew louder as it closed the gap between them.

He raced over to Cordelia and refired the warm engine. She enthusiastically spun her rotors as gray fumes spit from her exhaust. She looked pissed off but ready to go.

Cordelia sprung from her perch as all four propellers achieved lift. She throttled up in a perfectly straight ascent, leaving the Canadian with no second thought or remorse. In four seconds, the tall trees were looking up at the little quadcopter, watching her climb until she was barely visible.

Cordelia hovered at the peak of her range. Her wide eye scanned the ground momentarily and then she turned her focus to the oncoming plane. She needed to be flawless. Her altitude perfect. Her timing impeccable. She had one chance to prove her worth.

Below, the Canadian's eyes burned into the monitor mounted on the remote control. He had picked this location after hours of calculating and planning. The Beechcraft would stay low without the altimeter working correctly, so he made sure it would fail while doing his routine maintenance. He also sabotaged the windshield wiper to obscure Ozzie's view and force him to fly by GPS to stay on course. The plane would still have been out of Cordelia's vertical limit, but the ridge he climbed to fulfill this mission increased his elevation by 700 feet. If Ozzy kept the plane at an altitude of -1,200 feet, Cordelia could easily reach him before she hit her vertical limit or left the remote control's range.

Finally, the plane came into sight. To Cordelia's surprise, it was lower than she had anticipated. She back-flipped and dove straight down until she was hovering about 500 feet off the ridge, and refocused. Thirty feet too low. A boost in throttle brought her back up again. She had one shot to win her game of chicken against the Beechcraft, which was closing in at almost 263 miles per hour. Cordelia yawed to the left, pitched forward, and sped 70 feet. She was fast and extremely agile, like a cat chasing a laser pointer. Now, her alignment was nearly perfect. The homemade pipe bomb pointed straight at the propeller of the incoming aircraft. Just a few more seconds of patience and she would prove her loyalty to her creator watching below.

Ozzy Sullivan squinted through the beads of water condensing on the cold windshield. The wiper was nearly useless, but the wind was blowing the condensation off the top and sides as the Beechcraft's aerodynamics worked flawlessly. He looked back to see Blankenship reading a magazine with a pistol on the front cover. The case of money lay on the copilot's seat. Ozzy thought about the pistol holstered on his side—a Taurus .38 special revolver. He could easily pull the gun now, dispatch the brutish bodyguard and fly away with the loot. It would be easy.

Or would it?

Blankenship was to report to Skiff as soon as the wheels hit the ground. If he did not call, Skiff had more associates he could contact to find the plane. The fuel gauge vibrated from the roaring engine, making it difficult to get an accurate reading, but he knew there would be little excess fuel for this trip. The plane would make it to Schenectady and then to Burlington, plus a little further if an emergency arose. How far could he get? Not very. He'd have to ditch the plane in some farmer's field and go on the run. He hadn't prepared for that.

"Damn," he thought to himself, "should've planned this before we left." He gave up on the fantasy, knowing full well he could not pull off such a heist and live to tell about it. It wasn't worth the risk, and he wasn't ready to die for Skiff's dirty money. "Maybe next time," he thought.

He turned his attention back to the sky and scenic mountains appearing in his trajectory. He'd wished it was Fall and the curvaceous peaks in his foreground were yellow, orange, and red. Without the canopy of leaves, Ozzy could see every detail of the terrain below—the rocks, creeks, and beaver ponds. He could see whitetail-deer browsing the hillsides and flocks of winter birds scuttering about the trees. A murder of crows, perched in a large tree overlooking an unplowed road, scattered as the plane flew overhead. When his keen eyes left the ground and leveled out in front of the plane, he saw the anomaly in the sky hovering directly in the plane's path. Cordelia stared him down like some maniacal killer in a horror movie.

"What the bloody…holy shit!"

Ozzy cranked the yoke to the right, stepped on the rudder pedal, and hammered the throttle. The Beechcraft responded and banked. Cordelia's all-seeing eye saw the evasive maneuver and countered. A straight shot was out of the question now. Cordelia yawed to the left 30 degrees, anticipated the new flight path, and bolted forward. She screamed like a warrior—all four rotors spinning at full speed as she launched her Kamikazee assault.

Ozzy couldn't see the quadcopter outside becausing he was banking away. He changed rudder and direction to level out again but stayed on the throttle so the plane could climb in altitude. His eyes nearly burst out of his head when he realized the drone had turned and was tracking the plane. He knew the plane would take some damage, but he had no idea how bad it would be.

Blankenship heard the terror in Ozzy's scream and instinctively grabbed his assault rifle.

Cordelia zipped at almost 70 miles per hour. The Beechcraft had no further evasive tricks and held its course. Cordelia was aiming straight for the engine mounted at the front of the plane, but the plane was faster than she realized. Milliseconds before the collision the light button was flipped to the 'on' position sending the electric current from Cordelia's battery pack to the canister. The spark lit the gunpowder, which exploded with the force of dynamite. Two-hundred ball bearings exploded out the weak end of the canister and into the Beechcraft. They violently tore through the thin metal of the plane, piercing the fuselage and perforating the frame. They ripped apart fuel lines, punctured the engine block, devastated the door and its hinges, shred the left wing, and left a hole in the plane the size of a hoolahoop. The ball bearings ricocheted within the interior of the plane, creating more destruction.

The bomb destroyed Ozzy's left leg. He felt nothing, however, as one of the steel balls struck beneath his chin as he turned his face away. It had blasted into his head, slowing on impact and bounced around inside his skull, tearing his brain apart. The Irish pilot was dead.

Chapter 9 / *Too Loud to be a Rifle*

The northern pikes were ravenous that morning, swallowing minnow after minnow and the Marten brothers couldn't have been happier. They took turns chasing triggered flags and pulling lunkers through the fishing holes.

"Damn," Paul said. "Haven't seen a day of fishing this good in years."

"I know," Jack replied. "If this keeps up, we'll be out of minnows by noon."

"That's a good problem to have," Paul said. "Andy looks like he's having some luck. How many has he got, Eric?"

Eric had just returned from chatting with Andy. The big man was still sitting at the same hole, jigging for perch. "He's caught 11 perch, but he's thrown them all back."

Paul seemed a little puzzled. Andy lived off the land. Why wouldn't he keep the delicious perch after sitting there for almost two hours?

Paul finished rebaiting a hook, bent the spring-loaded flag down and hooked it on the trigger mechanism. Satisfied with his work, he scanned his surroundings, taking in the beauty of the Adirondack foothills and stillness of the world that enveloped him in cool white. He wished Stacie were here. He realized he hadn't thought about her since his feet hit the ice. This day was too perfect not to share with the woman he loved, and she enjoyed fishing with him as long as the weather was nice.

The grumbling from his stomach interrupted his thought, so he decided it was a good time to grab something from his cooler. His heavy boots thumped their way across the ice as he walked toward his jet sled parked by the fire. Eric must have had the same idea because he munched on an apple while he poked the fire. Paul turned one last time to check on his tip-ups before he got too far away. Jack, kneeling on the ice, was tending to a tangled line on the far side of the bay.

An eagle soared over their heads just 40 feet above the river. Paul's ungloved hand searched the depths of a front pocket, retrieving a cell phone and snapped a quick picture of the graceful raptor before it went out of sight. He reviewed the images—a little blurry, but a nice reminder of the day to add to the numerous pictures of he and his brothers with their fish.

Two bars were illuminated on his phone, indicating weak cell service. Paul took advantage of the rare signal strength and sent a text message to Stacie—*Hi Hon. Been a great day. Lots of fish. How's your day going?*

With the message sent, Paul stayed where he was standing as if his boots had frozen to the ice. Stepping in any direction might have meant losing the signal and not receiving a response from his wife. He waited.

That's when they heard it. A boom in the distance so violent that it seemed to knock snow off the surrounding evergreens. Jack spun on his knees and looked back at Paul.

"Thunder?" the eldest brother asked. He didn't need to yell. Sound traveled across the open bay well enough to hear a whisper.

"Too loud to be a rifle," Paul said.

Andy stood at attention from the interruption. He grabbed his metal chair and folded it up as if he were scared lighting would strike him. He tucked the chair neatly into his jet sled and hooked the fishing line on the little pole to an eyelet in the handle.

Paul listened intensely for another explosion—it never came. Instead, he heard the buzzing of an airplane engine as it sputtered and popped, approaching their location with great speed.

He expected to see the plane fly by at a low altitude, but instead, he heard trees snapping beyond Jack, and without warning, the crippled Beechcraft burst through the treetops directly over Jack's head. Snow rained down on Jack who had no time to move or react.

The left wing of the plane collided with a stout pine tree, severing the wing at its midpoint. The bulk of the wing spiraled through the air, just missing Jack. The impact spun the plane 20 degrees and caused it to veer between Paul and Andy. Fire and smoke billowed from the engine as it completely died. For an instant, all was quiet, until the white plane smacked nose first onto the hard ice, breaking through and leaving a four-foot wide hole. It bounced nine feet into the air and came down with another hard impact. The plane slid across the ice as Paul and Andy split directions and shuffled as fast as they could, trying to gain traction on the slick ice underfoot. Paul dove to the ice to avoid the plane's right wing, and knocked the wind from his lungs as he landed on his chest. Andy tripped over his sled, spilling its contents for the second time that day. The momentum of the 2,000-pound aircraft caused it to keep skidding across the bay with the sound similar to a dumpster being dragged down a blacktop road.

The plane rotated and tried to roll, but the intact wing kept it upright. With the right wing now digging into the ice, the tip of the wing acted like the blade of a hockey skate and steered the wreckage toward the thinner ice of the tributary brook. Finally, whether it was friction or the loss of momentum, the plane stopped. The thinner ice had claimed the life of a deer two years ago and nearly took Eric's life that same year. Now, it was hungry for something more. Ice cracked and spidered under the weight of the plane. At first, it was hard to determine if the water was gushing onto the ice, or if the ice was sinking. The latter turned out to be true, and with one final crack, the plane broke through with a loud hiss as the hot engine and fire met the cold water of the Raquette River. The front of the plane sank fast into the 12 feet of water, leaving the tail resting on the solid ice that remained. The tail of the plane protruded from the water with its two tail wings forming a cross—a tombstone marking a grave.

Eric and Jack were already running out to check on Paul and Andy. Paul's heart was pounding against his Carhart overalls as he stood on his knees watching in disbelief.

"What the hell?" Jack exclaimed upon approaching. "You okay?"

Paul nodded and looked at Andy, who was laying on his back, propped up on his elbows with a big smile on his face. Paul figured he was happy for the excitement.

"You okay, Andy?" Paul shouted too loud.

"Hehe, yeah, I'm okay. Sonovabitch in the plane ain't, though."

"We've got to see if anyone's on board!" Eric shouted as he met his brothers.

"Pilot's dead," Paul said. "I could see him clearly through the windshield. Looked like…" He stopped, not wanting to describe what he had witnessed. "Shit. Let's go look." He wasn't sure if it was the right thing to do, or the adrenaline talking, but they all agreed.

Andy stood and brushed the snow off his green wool coat. "Hehe, did you see that? I near shit my tighty-whities," The big man had snow covering his beard and eyebrows from his intimate moment with the cold powder. He brushed his coat and face with a mittened hand.

"I'll grab my fishfinder," Jack said. "Maybe we can get a view of what's inside." He sprinted toward the fire, where he'd left his fishing gear, to retrieve the device.

Paul and Eric sprinted toward the wreckage. Eric stopped 20 yards short of the mess and held his left arm out like a boom gate in a parking garage. "This is where the ice gets pretty thin." Eric dropped to his knees and started brushing the ice with thick buckskin mittens. The ice was still white and looked dense, but they had to consider if the plane had compromised its integrity. Eric shouted back to Jack, "Grab an ice spud!"

Jack, with his fish viewer tucked under his arm like a football, had just started on his way back when he got the request. His feet slid three feet across the ice when he tried to stop and reverse direction. The ice spud was five feet long and built from a three-quarter inch steel bar. It had a three-inch wide steel chisel welded to one end, and a T-handle welded to the other. Fishermen used the ice spud to test the thickness and hardness of the ice. As a fisherman walks, he continually taps the ice in front of himself with the seven pound tool. With experience, he acquires the ability to gauge the depth of the ice just by the sound the spud makes as it strikes the surface. The duller the sound, the thicker the ice. If the spud broke through the ice, then it would not be capable of supporting a man's weight. The ice spud was also useful for chipping away any ice forming around tip-ups, and to roughen the ice to increase traction under their boots. It was a useful tool that went on every ice fishing excursion with them.

While they waited for Jack to return to the site of the crash, Paul watched Andy trying to reload his gear back into the jet sled. Andy was mouthing something into his walkie-talkie. He then stuffed the electronic into the bottom of his pack basket and continued organizing his gear.

"Good," Paul sighed. "Andy's reporting the crash to whoever's on the other end of that line."

Jack's jog turned into a hastened walk as he returned to his brothers and the crash. Breathing hard, he unzipped his jacket and let the air cool his overheated body. Eric took the fish viewer from Jack and handed the ice spud to Paul. It was Eric's way of refusing to go near the hole in the ice.

Paul gripped the metal spud in his right hand and kept his arm extended in front of himself as he began testing the surface they depended on to support their weight. He tapped the ice to his right, then in front, and to his left. The sound was dull and solid. Peeking over his shoulder, Paul looked at Jack.

"Six, maybe seven inches," Jack said. Jack was more experienced than his brothers. Hell, he was more experienced at ice fishing than anyone they knew—except for maybe Andy Kessler, who didn't work a full-time job and relied on the river to sustain his life.

A couple more steps and Paul tapped again. The ice was healthy here, too. Two more steps and they were less than ten yards from the plane's tail protruding from the ice. The three brothers walked in single file and maintained four feet between them. Paul was now eight feet from the hole the plane had created. The ice was four inches at this point, which was plenty thick enough to support their weight. However, they were not sure of the ice's integrity and maintained a cautious approach. The ice popped and cracked but stayed intact, and the three Martens maintained the four feet of space between them to keep their weight distributed.

Eric was the most nervous. The area was where he'd nearly lost his life two years ago, saved only by the poor fate of a trophy whitetail buck. He kept his attention on the fish viewer, pushing the traumatic memory into a vault within his mind. Now was not the time to let such a thing surface. He drowned the memory and opened the fish viewer.

The fish viewer was stored in a yellow plastic case the size of a laptop computer but eight inches thick. Eric took the lens from its custom formed foam rubber bed. The unit looked like a little submarine with the front quarter cut away and replaced with a glass lens encircled by a dozen light-emitting diodes. Two metal ballast, resembling CO_2 cartridges, ran the length of both sides to balance the lens. The submersible lens wasn't much bigger than a potato and tethered by a whip of fiber optic and copper wires that snaked back to the yellow case. An LCD monitor was mounted in the top of the case, only visible when the container was open. A couple of controls to zoom and turn the lens and a rechargeable battery completed the ensemble.

Jack lit a menthol. "Battery looks good." He was on his knees watching the LCD screen, but all he saw so far was Paul unwinding the tether. "Take a little more, so you've got some slack in the line."

Paul walked the little camera out to the left edge of the giant hole created by the ill-fated plane. He let the camera sink as Jack and Eric watched the monitor. Peering into the eight-inch screen was like looking into another world. A world with rich sandy soil and the occasional rock adorning the terrain and wavy trees of seaweed dancing in the current. It was difficult to get a sense of scale in this alien world until a smallmouth bass swam curiously close to the camera's eye. The 12-inch fish vanished under the wreckage which lay nose first in the sand.

On the fragile surface of the ice, Jack and Eric stared at the monitor. "Bring it back up about two feet," Jack directed Paul.

Paul pulled the tether like he had a small trout on the end of the line—gingerly keeping the line taught trying not to let the little trout shake the hook. The camera reached the cockpit window where a green flight jacket was visible. "A little more," Eric requested, hardly believing the command and knew he was about to see the face of the deceased pilot.

The ice cracked under Jack and Eric's knees, sending a small shockwave through their hips. They jumped back and to their feet with the speed of a professional wrestler. The ice was thin in this area, and when Andy added his weight to the surface, it buckled and cracked. Jack and Eric spun around to see Andy peeking over their shoulders, attempting to see what was on the little monitor. Jack made a motion at Andy with his hand to back up. Andy took a few steps away from the monitor, moving his weight away from the area of ice that began to crack.

"That's pretty friggin cool," the big man grinned. "Look at the fish down there."

"Jesus, Andy, there's a dead man down there, maybe more," Jack snapped.

"Sorry. Never looked under the ice before. Kinda awesome, hehe."

The monitor finally showed the damage to the plane as the LED lights illuminated the white plane. The engine cowl had a hole that was similar in size to a backpack and shaped like North Carolina. Holes, of many different sizes, perforated the plane's exterior, and the fire from the engine had left the side of the plane charred. The pilot was small in stature and his clothes tattered and burned. The shape of his face indicated severe bone fractures as it drooped to the right—the left, bloody and torn, was missing a cheek. The brothers grimaced and slightly turned away at the scene, hoping he was the only casualty on board.

"What is it?" Paul asked when he saw their faces. Before anyone could answer, Andy turned and dry-heaved. "Nevermind," Paul said, "Don't think I wanna know."

They scanned the outside of the plane a little more. The fuselage and engine compartment were riddled with holes of various sizes. Eric's face moved closer to the monitor and raised his sunglasses to rest on his head. He squinted at the screen for a moment.

"Those holes don't have any burrs protruding out," he said. "And each hole is inside a concave dent."

"So they were created from the outside. Like bullet holes," Jack said.

"Yeah. But we only heard one explosion. Whatever shot this plane down had massive power."

"Holy shit, fellas," Andy interrupted. "You saying this is from a bomb? Somebody blew this thing out of the sky?"

"Appears that way," Jack answered. "Question is: who and why?"

"That's two questions, hehe" Andy smiled.

They guided the little camera back toward what used to be the left wing and peered into the window. The LED lights lit the interior of the plane giving them an eerie view of two rear bucket seats. The double doors on the opposite side were open—the forward door looked skewed on its hinges, but the rear door was completely gone. Tree bark was embedded in the door frame, indicating it had already been ripped off while crashing through the trees. If anyone else had been on the plane, they were surely ripped through the open doors and killed on landing.

"Guys, look," Paul said. He was pointing to the surface of the water. Jack and Eric couldn't see from their position, so they walked over to Paul. They peeked over his shoulder and followed his finger, pointing at a $100 bill floating in the water and a couple more submerged below.

"Bet it's drug money," Paul said. "I'll bet this explains *why* the plane was shot down."

"It's our money, now," Jack smiled.

Chapter 10 / *Excelsior*

The Canadian was satisfied with Cordelia's work. Her sacrifice and loyalty had crippled the plane better than he expected. He had hoped the plane would drop quicker, but the little Beechcraft was determined to stay aloft for several more minutes, clawing and fighting her way across the sky, like a wounded soldier pulling himself across a battlefield and not willing to give up on life.

The Canadian put the remote control away and thought about the horror on Ozzy's face before Cordelia discharged the pipe bomb. His heart felt like a sandbag in his chest. He was genuinely sorry for what he had to do—for what he'd done. Ozzy was an acquaintance, unlike Moonie Swamp, whom he had not known for more than 90 minutes. If he returned to his job as a mechanic at the airport, he would face Ozzy's friends every day and be hiding the guilt of his murder deep in his chest. The lie would eat away at him physically and emotionally, creating constant stress, and making him grow old all too quickly. He could never return to his job, to Canada, or to his home, even if he failed to acquire the money on that plane. But, returning home was never in his plan, anyway.

A squawk came over his two-way radio, startling him back to reality. He had forgotten he was even carrying the damn thing. He was happy for the interuption to his thoughts, and removed the red walkie-talkie from a cargo pocket in his pants and turned the volume down, even though no one was within miles of hearing him.

"Yeah, I'm here. Did you see it go down?" the Canadian asked the individual on the sister radio.

"Hehe, hell yes I saw it go down. You nearly dropped the damn thing on my head," the voice responded enthusiastically, but softly.

"Good. What's your location?"

"I'm on the river. Follow the road for a couple of miles until you see a giant rock, like 12 feet high. Its shaped like a big haystack. Cut into the woods on the right, just past the rock. You'll see my tracks in the snow. Follow 'em to the river. You can't miss it."

"Great, give me about 45 minutes. Grab the money if you can, but be careful, just in case the security guard survived. You don't want to mess with him."

"Uh...see, that's gonna be a problem."

"Why? What the hell are you talking about, eh?"

"Well, hehe, the plane landed on the bay, and then it went into the bay. So the whole thing is in the drink."

"Its in the water?"

"Yup."

The Canadian wanted to scream. He balled his hand into a fist, looking for something to punch, but there was nothing. Of all the places the wreckage could have smacked down, it had to be in the friggin water. He shook the fist loose and took a breath. "Can we get to it somehow? You must have some equipment at your cabin we could use."

"Yeah, well, that's not the only problem. I'm not alone. There're three brothers here, too—local boys. They've been ice fishing this bay all morning, and now they're going to look at the plane."

"Sonavabitch! Did they report it?" the Canadian asked.

"No, no, there's no cell phone service out here."

"Okay. Good. Okay. I'm on my way. Don't let them leave if they get that money. Over and out." The Canadian hastened his organization, packed up the quadcopter case—minus the quadcopter—snuffed the fire, and folded a white tarp he'd strung in the trees for camouflage.

He had prepared for this contingency, knowing he might cross paths with some snowmobilers, hikers, or fishers while he and Andy searched for the downed plane. He unzipped the large backpack he was lugging around and rummaged through the contents. He thought about Moonie's words. "That's a pretty big bag in the back. I mean, if the cops see ya huffing with that, they're gonna run you down." He realized the kid was right, but fortunately, he was not spotted during his illegal journey.

He pulled out his pistol to check it. Three men were all that stood between him and his money. Hopefully, they would leave the scene and go home to their normal lives without incident. Hopefully, they were smarter than Moonie and wouldn't fuck with him. If they became suspicious or problematic, he would have no choice but to end their existence.

102

He racked a .357 caliber bullet into the chamber of his SIG 226 pistol and peeked down the sights. He holstered the pistol to his right hip. The holster was attached to a heavy utility belt that encircled his waist and was also home to a small flashlight, an empty canister of pepper spray, and a set of toy handcuffs to make the costume more believable. He retrieved a heavy green coat. Not the green of grass or a color similar to the Jeep he had driven here, but an earthy color that reminded the Canadian of his days in the Army.

He studied the patches embroidered on the coat's shoulders for the first time. The patches were black with yellow text, reading "New York State Environmental Conservation/Police." A couple of women wearing robes were embroidered on the patch. The woman on the left was armed with a spear while the other held a set of scales—Liberty and Justice. Justice, holding the scales, wore a blindfold to cast her judgment fairly and without prejudice. The Canadian laughed at the image, realizing he could sneak a stack of cash on one side of those scales without her noticing, to tip the scales in his favor. They stood next to a scene of a ship sailing a river with an eagle displayed above. A banner across the bottom held a single Latin word which he read out loud, "Excelsior."

He stood on the ridge and scanned the horizon to the north where some dark cumulus clouds were dumping two inches of snow per hour. The storm was predicted to stay north of his location as it traveled from west to east. Lake Ontario had not frozen over this year, causing the wide storm to pick up moisture and carry it to the mountains. As the clouds rose higher into the Adirondacks, the moisture dropped in the form of snow. The weather was working in the Canadian's favor—slowing any rescue vehicles on their way to the crash. The weather was also forcing most people to stay home and forego any recreational activities today, so he wouldn't have to worry about hikers snowshoeing, cross-country skiers, or automobiles. It was possible that he would encounter some snowmobilers out riding—they were die-hards that wouldn't give a shit about the storm. Most fishermen would skip going to the ice today—most, except for three.

"Excelsior."

He began his two-mile hike to the bay to meet up with Andy and retrieve his money—"my money" as he called it now. He felt he had earned it. He traveled from Ottawa, braved the ice of the St. Lawrence River, took the life of Moonie Swamp, stole two vehicles, climbed this ridge, and sacrificed little Cordelia. Now, he just needed to put the prize in his hands.

He descended the ridge, weaving through the deciduous trees and back-tracking his way to the gravel road. The backpack was lighter without Cordelia in her case. Soon, he would be free of its bulk, and stash it in the woods near the stolen Jeep. He could return later to retrieve the pack, if necessary.

He finally hit level ground and could see the bright green Jeep 90 yards away. It stood out like a pea on a wedding cake. Snow had accumulated on the stolen Jeep's hood, roof, and bumpers, making it almost impossible to see from the air. Surely, the Jeep had been reported stolen by now, but the snow-covered trees had swallowed it up, concealing it from the rest of the world.

Snow started falling again. Large flakes, the size of dimes gliding on light currents of air. It was not a deluge of white, but a beautiful display of occasional flakes, like each one took its turn jumping from the clouds above. They were misguided wanderers from the edge of the storm. The air temperature was slightly on the rise as well, causing the flakes to stick together as they collided in mid-air.

The Canadian looked to the sky, allowing some of the large flakes to cool his face. He felt warm from the hike down the hill, and for a moment, he was lost in the precipitation's hypnotic influence, even sticking his tongue out like a kid to catch a few in his mouth. In his mind, he was nine again, ice-skating on the Rideau Canal with his brother and mother. He could smell the hot dog stand and hear the kids laughing. The sound of hockey pucks slapping against hardwood sticks echoed in his eardrum. He could feel the vibrations as he skated over thousands of little fissures made by thousands of sharp blades. He and his brother would skate for miles on the canal, often leaving their mother on her own to gossip with vendors and other moms. She didn't mind. She wanted them to go far, follow a path of their own, and be brave. They always returned to find her in the same warming room, rubbing her feet that were sore and swollen from the tight figure skates, but she never complained about the discomfort or the cold. She made whatever sacrifices she had to for her children. She was a good mom.

What would she think of him now?

The image of the canal morphed into a snowy field, and the hotdog stand and benches were replaced by hundreds of tombstones. The skaters were now mourners, scouring the cemetery politely as they read the names engraved in stone. Snow covered the headstone at his feet. Yellow daffodils peeked through the snow, defying the winter weather. A hummingbird sipped the nectar of the yellow flower, then froze in place—stuck there forever as if the headstone was his.

The Canadian opened his eyes wide, ingesting the visual reality that was. He smelled moss and bark and wet gravel, but no daffodils. The sound of the hummingbird disappeared. It was refreshing to be back to reality.

He was thirsty. The exertion of the hike had exhausted and dehydrated his body, so the Canadian rummaged through his backpack for a bottle of water. The ice-cold liquid soothed his raw throat and revitalized his muscles. No more daydreaming. No more visions.

Time to go.

He stashed the backpack beside the road, rather than in the Jeep. If the Jeep were recovered, then he would still have his pack. He opted not to drive up the road, so he went to the vehicle and pulled out the keys. He didn't want anyone to recover the stolen vehicle or drive it up the road to catch him. He stuffed the keys in his pocket and began hiking. Stealth and surprise were on his side. He would give the fishermen a chance to retrieve the money and then take it from them. That was the plan. Andy could give him a ride later to pick up his backpack.

The walking was so much easier on the road than it was while tramping through the woods. Until this morning, the gravel road had not been used in months, except for a few snowmobiles that packed a solid base that would last until the next thaw. It was a four-mile hike to the bay where Andy was waiting, and he needed to get there before the three interlopers retrieved the money and got away. He headed south on Garrison Road; just himself and a set of tire tracks from earlier this morning. He followed Paul's tire tracks, like a hobo walking along the railroad, and hoped he wouldn't be too late.

Chapter 11 / *A Gut Feeling*

Bettinger Airport was eerily quiet after the white plane with red wings departed. The next flight for the day, scheduled for 12:50 pm, was canceled since the plane that was supposed to make the flight became stranded in Burlington, Vermont. The storm coming off Lake Ontario inched its way across the state, looking like a pink slug on the radar screen. It lumbered its way from west to east, leaving its cold white slime covering the ground between the airport and Bear Bay—dividing Stacie and Paul.

Stacie had called Border Patrol 30 minutes ago to report Officer Greene's strange transaction with plane C-FBZA. The grumpy woman on the other end of the call informed her she could only report a problem to the supervisor, who was attending a crime scene on the reservation. She left her name and number and awaited his return call.

Stacie was scheduled to stay at the airport until 5:00 p.m., whether or not there were passengers or flights. Her phone blinked silently in the quiet break room where she was reading a book on her kindle about pregnancy. Normally, she preferred a good paperback book with its distinct smell, tangible pages, and the satisfaction of seeing how much she'd read in a day. But for this topic, she could discretely bone up on topics of morning sickness, unexpected bleeding, and baby's first night home, without anyone knowing about her little secret.

She finally noticed the phone beckoning her to read its message. She thought she'd missed a call from the Border Patrol supervisor but was happy to see it was a text message.

107

Paul's message brought a smile to her face. She hadn't expected to hear from him all day since there was no cell service where he was fishing. She typed in her response and hit the send button.

Message not sent.

"Dang."

Her delicate thumb pushed the send button again. The result was the same.

A noise from the other side of the office stole her attention. It was the chirp of an incoming email. She opened the email from the Sheriff's department and then clicked on the attached PDF file. The file opened, and Stacie printed it at the printer adjacent to her desk. When the printer finally spit out the document, she walked into the breakroom and pinned it on the bulletin board for all the employees to see.

"Be On the Look Out:

Male / Possible Canadian citizen.

Name: Unkown

Height: 5' 11" / Weight: 210lbs

Hair: Red / Red Beard

Eyes: Blue

Wanted for questioning related to a homocide on the St. Regis Mohawk Reservation.

Warning: Considered armed and dangerous. Do NOT approach.
Call the Sheriff's office, SRM Tribal Police, or 911 if located."

Stacie stared at a crewd sketch of the man on the BOLO report. It was based on the description Kim had given the police after she had found Moonie's body. Kim wished she hadn't been so shy around the Canadian and had gotten a better look at his face.

Stacie read all the details but knew she wouldn't see the Canadian today since there were no flights. She wondered if, somehow, the Canadian was aboard the plane that Greene had lazily inspected this morning. Then she realized that didn't make much sense. The man on the BOLO report was already in the country before the plane landed. But still, she couldn't help but think the two events were related.

She stretched, reaching for the ceiling with interlocked fingers. For the first time, she felt a tightness in her lower abdomen that wasn't there a few days ago. Her delicate fingers caressed the little bump forming below her navel.

She smiled.

Then, she smiled some more.

Forgetting about the BOLO, Officer Greene, and work, she snatched up her computer bag, stuffed the Kindle into it and headed for the door. When she passed the ticket counter, Daryl was polishing the granite counter to keep himself occupied.

"Bye, Daryl. I'm taking personal time for the rest of the day."

"Might as well. No more flights today," Daryl responded. "I'm gonna leave at noon. See you Tuesday."

"See you Tuesday."

Stacie drove out of the parking lot and headed down Route 37. The stop light at the intersection of Routes 37 and 56 turned red, and she braked hard to heed its command. Straight would lead her home. Left would take her to Higley, to Bear Bay, and to Paul.

She thought about Paul's message. He seemed to be happy for the first time in weeks, and she couldn't wait to see his reaction when she finally told him the news.

"Aw, fuck it."

The car's left signal light came on, flashing as fast as the images in her brain of the two of them starting a family.

Family. The word seemed foreign to her. She had no family to share this news. Her parents, both deceased, would have turned this into a negative situation. They'd tell her how irresponsible she was, and that they couldn't afford to have a baby right now. They'd tell her how expensive diapers and formula would be, and ask who was going to watch the baby when she worked so much.

Uncle Ernie and Aunt Marie were all she had for family. They still resided in Higley but were planning to move to Georgia this spring, when Ernie retired from his job. They adored Stacie and treated her like a daughter. Stacie had even lived with them for a couple of summers as a teenager. Since they had two grown boys, she was the only girl in their lives and had always kept in touch.

Her sister lived in Florida. "Somewhere" was the only address she had for her. They hadn't spoken in eight years unless she counted the time her older sister called to see if mom and dad had left her anything in their will.

No. No, they had no will. They had no money, and they had no fucking will. Stacie paid off their debts and paid for their funeral expenses. She dropped out of college to work full time to cover the expenses. It took her four years to recover from the downturn and start saving money again. You're all very fucking welcome.

She turned the car left when the light turned green and drove south instead of west. The thought of her parents and sister upset her. Driving to Higley, seeing the man she loved and the aunt and uncle that adored her was just what she needed. She couldn't wait any longer to tell Paul her news. The day was still young—she could be there before noon—and she knew her way to Bear Bay. Paul was going to be so surprised to see her and to hear the news.

The Subaru steered toward the thick dark clouds on the horizon. They looked like the offensive line of a football team, in dull gray and white uniforms, waiting at the line of scrimmage. They were ready to block her with their curtain of white snow and blowing wind. Most drivers avoided the route today, except one pregnant little linebacker who was determined to push through.

She cautiously drove the all-wheel-drive car toward the storm. The window was down an inch to let the fresh winter air circulate within the car. She turned the volume up just as the local news started to broadcast. The news anchor reiterated what the BOLO report had announced, but a new development had occurred in the last few minutes that wasn't on the report. Police had found Moonie's truck, which they knew the killer had stolen, at a bar in Higley. They were now searching for a stolen green Jeep.

Chapter 12 / *Officer Dumbass*

After finding a few $100 bills and fishing them out of the water, the Marten brothers jockeyed the fish viewer around to the other side of the downed plane. They ignored the two flags that had popped on their tip-ups. The bright orange flags beckoned them to come to the hole and reel in the cold-blooded fish hooked below the ice. The fish viewer made its way around the plane continuing its investigation. Darkness swallowed the lens momentarily as the battery neared the end of its life and Jack and Eric stared a blank screen.

"The battery is dying," Eric said to Paul. "We might as well pull the camera out."

Paul raised the camera a few feet when the lights kicked back on. The camera stopped, stuck on the broken glass of the copilot's window. Paul gave the camera a little tension, trying to free it from the glass shards. He needed to avoid slashing the tether against the broken window, so he kept the tension on the line. The camera flickered back to life, and the monitor's pixels illuminated again.

"Whoa!" shouted Jack. "Pull a little bit more, so the camera tips downward, Paul."

Paul followed his brother's command.

"There it is. Jackpot," Eric said.

"Whatta ya see?" Paul asked.

Andy was hovering over their shoulders. He was quiet until now, watching the brothers work the little camera gingerly around the wreckage. "Looks like a case sitting on the floor in the cockpit."

"A case of money? Or a case of beer?" Paul asked.

"Well, if it's a case of money, we can buy all the beer we want," Jack replied.

"So, now what?" Andy asked. "That may not be money, and that dag-gone thing is in 12 feet of water…maybe more."

"Andy's right," Eric said. "I think we just need to head back to town and report this. Somebody's got to be looking for this plane."

"Fuck, Eric," Jack said. "If this plane had been reported missing, the search parties would be here by now."

"Only if they knew where it went down. We're in the middle of nowhere, and these are big woods to search. We're surrounded by 19 thousand acres of state forest."

"When was the last time we saw anybody out here other than Andy? We've got plenty of time to check this thing out before anyone comes along."

Eric looked at Paul for back-up. Paul, lost in thought, peered into the water as if he could will the case to him. His brain was burning with ideas. There were so many ways he could benefit from the money that could be inside that case. If the case was full of money, all of his and Stacie's financial problems would be resolved. They could pay off her student loans and both vehicles.

They'd have to be careful not to deposit the money in a bank so the I.R.S. wouldn't be aware of their new found fortune that fell out of the sky, almost killing him.

"Let's think about this," Paul finally said as Jack and Eric argued. Paul pulled the camera's tether and reeled the little camera hand-over-hand until it emerged from the dark water. They worked to put the camera back in its case while they weighed their options. Then the four of them huddled around the camera case. Jack pulled out a pack of menthols and offered one to everybody. Paul accepted.

"Two of us want to retrieve that money," Paul said.

"We don't even know if it is money in the case," Eric interrupted. "For all we know, it could be a box of Playboys."

"Hehe, might be worth getting after all," Andy chuckled.

"It's not worth risking our lives," Eric continued. "I've been down there, remember? There's a current that will drag you right under the ice." He made a sweeping motion with his arm that ended with his index finger pointed toward the middle of the bay. "Even you can't swim that well, Paul. I don't care how much money might be down there—it's not worth your life."

"Maybe we can jerry-rig something to fish it out," Jack said.

"Maybe a fishing line and a depth-finder," Paul added. "If we can get a hook through that window…"

"Window looked too small," Jack said, holding his hands about 18 inches apart. He realized that Paul could not see the monitor since he was manning the tethered camera. "I think the case is wider than the window. We'll have to, somehow, bring the case through the cargo doors."

"There's only one way to get it," Eric said, "And I don't think it's a good idea. Somebody would have to swim through those broken cargo doors, and it sure the hell isn't going to be me."

"Andy?" Paul looked at the mountain-man. "If I retrieve that case, would you mind if we go back to your cabin to dry off and warm up?" Paul and his brothers knew Andy's cabin was only a half-mile from the bay. They just needed to cut through the woods and get back on the Garrison Road. They could be at his cabin in 30 minutes or less.

"Absolutely," the jolly man replied. "I got a fire going and a little Jim Beam to warm your ass. We can even fry up one of them fresh pikes to eat."

Paul looked at Jack questionably. Jack looked at Eric reassuringly. Eric looked concerned, and Andy looked at his cheap watch.

"Okay, I'll do it," Paul said. "I'll swim down there and grab the case, then we head straight to Andy's cabin and warm up."

"And split the money," Jack added.

Eric knew there was no sense in arguing the matter any further. Paul had made up his mind, and Jack was committed to the plan. Instead of arguing further, he thought about how he could help.

"Let's get our gear packed up, so we're ready to go as soon as I come out of the water," Paul said. They all nodded in agreement and headed back to the dying fire to get their jet sleds and start picking up the tip-ups scattered throughout the bay.

"You trust Andy?" Paul asked Jack as they made their way to shore.

"Yeah. Andy's a good guy. He's whacked on homegrown most of the time, but he doesn't talk to anyone. He'll keep his mouth shut about this."

"We'll have to explain to him about not spending it lavishly; keep it out of the bank and don't make any big purchases."

"You think Andy's the type to buy Cuban cigars, a fancy yacht, and a vacation home in the Keys?" Jack laughed.

"No, but he is the type to go to town and buy a new truck, some rifles, and a few rounds at the bar."

"That's my plan," Jack said. "You should, too."

They fed the fire. Paul could use its heat when he emerged from the bottom of the river to stave off hypothermia. Then they'd make their way to Andy's cabin and dry out in his shelter by the fire. A couple ounces of Jim Beam sounded like an added bonus.

They dragged their jet sleds to the center of the bay and began pulling tip-ups out of the holes they had drilled. Paul noticed that one one of his tip-ups was already out of the water and smashed beyond repair. The remaining half of the right wing of the plane had annihilated the wooden fishing instrument. He lifted a couple of larger pieces of the splintered wood to inspect the damage. A total loss, he tossed the remnants into the bottom of his sled.

His thoughts drifted to the conversation he had with Stacie that morning. Could he start his own business if he retrieved the money? Would he need to? The thought of being his own boss became more appealing when he knew the risk was lower. But, if there were enough money in that case, maybe he'd never have to work again. That seemed impossible.

The ice popped under his feet, sounding like a Coke bottle breaking, and a crack opened up leading to a hole in the ice. For a second, he thought his plunge into the water would come earlier than planned as he felt the sheet of ice move under his weight. He side-stepped a couple of times until his feet hit slushy snow. Water was flooding the ice where he was standing. The plane had punched a hole through the ice when it first crashed down. For some reason, the ice was thinner here, perhaps the result of a sandbar pushing the current upward.

Paul backed up, putting some space between himself and the compromised ice.

He checked to be sure no one else was coming in this direction. Jack was further out toward the open water of the main channel. Eric was closer to shore on the south side. The broken tip-up was retrieved from the sled, and Paul set the flag near the hole to mark the danger. If anyone stepped too close, they would surely plunge into the river.

Andy was on his two-way radio again. He hadn't walked more than 12 feet from the plane, his conversation not audible to Paul.

"Hey, it's me," Andy spoke softly into the mirophone. "Can you hear me?"

"Yeah, yeah," the Canadian replied. "What's happening there?"

"Looks like they are going to dive in and get the money. One of the brothers has volunteered, and then we're going to my cabin to dry off and get warmed up. And we're going to drink some Jim Beam."

"Do you think they can do it?"

"Get the money? I think so. They seem pretty determined, but it is going to be dangerous."

"Okay. I'll be there soon. I'll make sure one of those boys goes after that case, whether they want to or not. Over and out."

Andy turned off the walkie-talkie and buried it in his pack basket. He hung his head for a moment with guilt. He thought about what was going to happen after the money was brought up from the bottom of the river. He thought about how much he enjoyed the company of the three men. He thought about what he could do with the money and honestly couldn't come up with much. He had everything he needed in life, didn't he? A cabin on the river, a dependable old truck, and a view of the Adirondack Mountains from his front porch.

He didn't have a woman in his life—never really had. Would money change that? Probably not. Maybe he'd just forfeit his percentage to the Canadian. Maybe he'd just give it to the Marten brothers. His head hurt from thinking about all of this as if his skull were cracked like the ice only 12 feet away. He didn't know what to do, so maybe he'd do nothing at all. Maybe he'd just leave.

Andy thought about why they were doing this. Their purpose was important—more important than money; more important than the Martens; more important than all their lives. He was convinced that this was for the greater good and that they must stick to the plan no matter what the outcome.

"All packed up?" Andy shouted to the three.

"Hell yeah," Jack shouted back. He was beaming with enthusiasm.

"Almost," Paul replied. "Eric? Whattabout you?"

Eric was pulling fishing line off the spools of his tip-ups. Each tip-up reel held about 100 feet of 20-pound test Spyder Wire fishing line. "Almost ready." He tied three of the lines to a small tree on shore. Each strand had been doubled up, and now he was braiding the three lines together. The braiding increased the tinsel strength even further, and when he finished, he had a 20-foot long rope with a tensile strength of 120 pounds. It was lighter than paracord, but Eric figured it would be enough to hold Paul's weight.

Paul and Jack were on their way to meet Eric by the fire. They watched Eric work on the makeshift rope and admitted it was a great idea. They arrived before Eric could finish the task and helped him with the last remaining braids. Eric took a lighter and burned both ends of the rope to melt the fibers together to prevent fraying.

"Ready," Eric said. He held the little rope up with a sense of pride, then coiled it around his left elbow and the palm of his hand, making a neat circle to prevent tangles. He tucked the coil in the large pocket of his jacket.

"Let's go," Eric said to the rest of the fisherman. The threesome started for the plane, but Eric stopped as if his boots had frozen to the ice. He pushed his sunglasses over his head. Young eyes scanned the pine trees, picking up movement within the shadows. He watched the figure walk toward them and onto the ice. "Change of plan," he announced. Paul and Jack saw his gaze fixed on the woods, and they followed Eric's eyes to the trail that had led them to Bear Bay.

"Is that Ernie?" Jack asked Paul. They could tell the man in uniform was from the Department of Environmental Conservation and Jack hoped it was Stacie's uncle.

"No," Paul said. "Ernie's taller. I don't recognize this guy. He might be a new officer."

Paul didn't know whether to feel relieved or upset as the figure approached them. Jack swore under his breath, visibly disappointed by the intrusion. Paul wondered if Andy had radioed someone from town who then called the authorities. That seemed unlikely, but it had been over an hour since the plane had crashed down.

The Canadian approached them with a fake smile on his face. His boots squeaked on the ice, sounding like a broken windshield wiper. His hands hid in the pockets of the jacket, which made him seem guarded and unsure of himself. The officer observed his surroundings, taking mental pictures of each fisherman and their actions. His eyes fixed on Paul and Jack, and he walked directly to their location. Eric continued on; making his way to the crash site and left Paul and Jack to explain everything.

"Watch that hole in the ice," Paul said, pointing to the first spot where the plane had punched through. The Canadian walked around the four-feet wide hole. Squeaky boots were silenced by the wet snow for a moment but commenced their squeaking when he exited the flooded area. His face was red as if he'd been out in the cold weather for some time. His red beard had tinges of frost which blended with the gray growing on his chin.

"Good day, gentlemen. How are you?" the Canadian asked.

"Good," Jack replied. "Nice day, ain't it?" Jack would have asked that question in a blizzard. To him, every day was nice, especially if he wasn't working.

"It's a gorgeous day. Storm in the north is pretty bad, but it looks like it's missing you guys," the Canadian said. "How's the fishing been?"

"Great," Paul said. "Until we were almost killed by a plane dropping out of the sky."

The D.E.C. officer did not seem amused. He nodded his head as if he'd heard all about it. "Yeah, I got a call about that. Thought somebody was pulling a joke on me or something. I gotta check it out though."

Paul shot a dirty look at Andy. He suspected he was right and that Andy was calling someone on the radio to report the crash. But, why didn't he just admit it? Andy didn't see Paul's glare since he stared down at the ice and at the plane's tail protruding from the water.

"Don't suppose there were any survivors by the looks of it," the Canadian observed.

"No. We tried to check," Jack admitted, nodding toward the fish viewer.

"We think the pilot was the only person on board," Paul added.

The fish viewer was still sitting on the ice, so the Canadian knew they had been trying to see the wreckage below. The men investigating the crash must not have seen Blankenship's body in the back of the plane. Maybe the big man was taken by the current or blown out of the plane by Cordelia's blast. His disdain for Blankenship had him hoping to see the bodyguard dead. Killing Ozzy was regrettable, but knocking Blankenship off was a bonus to the job.

"You guys have your fishing licenses?" The imposter asked. The question came out on its own. It was a sudden idea he had to acquire the Marten's names and addresses. Paul and Jack retrieved the requested documentation, and the Canadian filed the information mentally. "Thanks. Let's go see what kinda mess we've got, eh?"

The three of them walked to the plane, where Andy and Eric were already waiting.

"Got your fishing license?" the Canadian asked Eric. Eric complied, as his brothers had, and pulled his license from the front pocket of his Carhart overalls. "You guys brothers?" the Canadian asked as he handed Eric's license back.

"Yes, sir," Eric replied. "Except for Andy here. He lives just up-river." The Canadian nodded at Andy and turned toward the wreckage. He kicked a piece of debris that was sitting in the snow.

"Damn. What a friggin mess, eh? Might have to wait until spring to get that sonavabitch out."

"Might be easier while there is ice on," Jack said. "The ice is thick enough to drive a tractor on, as long as you don't get too close to this area. Is anybody on their way? Fire department? Police? Or just you?"

"No, I'm it for now. I'll have to call in for help when I get closer to town. Radio won't reach that far from here." He tapped on the red two-way radio fastened to his shoulder. "Guess there's no big rush since there are no survivors."

"Guess not," Paul said. He turned and walked away as if he'd lost interest in the whole situation. He took his phone out of his pocket, willing it with his mind to pick up a signal. Nothing. He tried to remember where he was standing before when he had a weak signal and was able to send a message to Stacie. He followed the plane's skid marks through the snow while studying his footprints. As he backtracked, he kept his phone raised above his head, hoping to see a bar light up on his phone to indicate reception.

"What's he doing?" The D.E.C. officer asked the others. He watched Paul wander away and keep his phone toward the sky.

"I think Paul had a signal out in the middle of the bay," Eric said. "Just before the plane crashed, he was able to send a text."

Paul stopped walking. He spun 90 degrees right, then 180 degrees left. Two bars lit up on the phone; then one; then back to two. The phone had picked up the elusive cell service again. With his arm out stretched, he held the phone with the camera pointing back at him—in 'selfie' mode. He could see himself, the plane's tail sticking out of the ice, and the group of men encircling it, on the phone's screen.

Click. Click. Click.

When he finished taking the selfies, he perused the photos, trying to decide which one to send to Stacie. He selected his choice and sent it with the message, "*Hi Hon. Been a crazy day here. Check this out. Leaving soon. Love you.*" He stayed in the same spot like a snowman, being sure not to move or lose the cell service. The weak signal would be slow to upload the file and send it through space, so he waited patiently. Squeaky boots approached him from behind.

"You can't be taking pictures of this crash," The D.E.C. officer said. His face turned redder, and there was a tone of annoyance in his voice.

"I just took a couple," Paul said. "Thought I'd send them to my wife while I've got cell service. She can call to report the plane crash."

"I'll need to see those pictures. This crash is still under investigation, and we can't leak anything until I notify the authorities."

"Well, my wife works at the airport for the Department of Homeland Security, so technically, she is an 'authority,'" Paul said. "She can run the serial number and identify the pilot for you."

"May I see the pictures?"

"Sure, I guess," Paul was the type of person who respected law enforcement. Even though something seemed off about this guy, Paul abided his request and scrolled through the last three pictures on his phone. They stood next to each other, shielding the screen from the glare of the sky.

"See, just a couple—"

The Canadian's powerful hand grabbed the phone and ripped it from Paul's grasp. The phone was tossed through the air and into the hole in the ice. With a splash, it disappeared, drifting to the bottom of the river with all of Paul's messages and photos. Paul was furious. He imagined the water dissolving pictures of Stacie from the phone's memory card. He had pictures of family, friends, ex-co-workers, and trips they had taken. There was a picture he'd taken of Stacie with some dolphins, that he wanted to print and frame. There was a picture of he and Dale Earnhardt, Jr. from a race at Pocono Speedway. There were pictures of their dog that died last summer. His rage snowballed as he thought about all the pictures, contacts, and messages he just lost.

He stared in disbelief at the watery hole that had just swallowed so much information. The phone lay at the bottom of the river now, and it would be impossible to retrieve. He would

126

have an easier time getting the case from the plane than acquiring his phone back.

Paul spun 180 degrees, "What the hell—!"

His words cut off from the sight in front of him. He stood nose to nose with a .357 pistol. Cold eyes stared down the sights at him, unpredictable and menacing. Paul stepped backed, raising his hands as a gesture that he was calm. He still wasn't sure why the officer was acting this way. Clearly, this man in uniform was a little unhinged and had an alternate agenda other than reporting the crashed Beechcraft.

"Move," the officer said, gesturing the gun toward the plane.

"Look, I didn't mean to—"

"Just move your ass."

Paul hiked over to the plane; squeaky boots followed with the pistol pushed against ribs. Paul could see the look of confusion on Jack and Eric's faces, even with their sunglasses donned. They watched quietly for a few moments as the D.E.C. officer marched Paul over at gunpoint.

"What the hell's going on?" Jack demanded. As the oldest brother, he always felt it was his responsibility to keep his younger brothers safe, but this was a whole new level of danger, and he felt helpless. Still, he was ready and willing to take a bullet for Paul or Eric if necessary.

"Officer dumbass didn't like me taking pictures for some reason," Paul said. His respect for the man with a gun had sunk with his phone. Paul felt a boot hit him in the middle of his back, knocking him forward and nearly on his face. Paul's experience on the ice kept him from falling from the blow. He stood straight again, composing himself and restraining his anger with every ounce of energy he had, but he was seething on the inside.

"All of you," the Canadian barked, "over here, or I put a bullet through your brother."

They were slow to move, unsure if they were doing the right thing. The Canadian put a bullet in the ice next to Paul's feet. The pistol was louder than he expected but Paul stood unfazed. Ice cracked from the lead bullet's impact but stayed sturdy. Andy jumped more than anyone. The big man's feet spun on the ice and then his upper body weight took over as he fell to his knees. He scrambled to get back up and joined the trio of brothers. He hid behind the Martens, like a kid in a classroom that hadn't finished his homework.

"What do you want?" Paul asked.

"There's something in that plane that belongs to me," the Canadian said as he removed his ball cap. "And one of you is going to go down there to get it."

Chapter 13 / *The Trail Less Traveled*

Stacie slowed the car to 28 miles per hour. The lights on the emergency vehicle up the road flashed blue while four road flares burned on the ground. She brought the Subaru to a stop in front of a thin young man flagging traffic on Route 56. The flashing was coming from a blue emergency light mounted on the dash of his truck. He was parked on the wrong side of the road, facing the oncoming traffic. The truck's intermittent windshield wipers swept right and then back to their original position. A couple of inches of snow had accumulated on the rest of the truck, indicating that it had been parked there for at least an hour.

Beyond the truck, Stacie could see more lights reflecting off the snowy trees and telephone poles, but the lights themselves were out of sight. These lights were a combination of red, blue, and orange, flashing in rapid succession. They were difficult to see during the daytime, but there was no mistaking them as emergency vehicle lights.

The young man was talking on a two-way radio. He spoke into the microphone and then listened for a reply. His head nodded up and down a couple of times as if the person on the other end could see him talking. Finally, he snapped the radio to his belt and came to the driver's side window as it receded into the car door.

"Good morning, ma'am," the young first responder greeted her. He was 18 years old with a smile as bright as the road flares. His baseball cap was ripped and torn on the bill, but Stacie decided it was designed to look that way. He had red cheeks from the cold, but only wore a hoodie and a pair of jeans. He was bare-handed and seemed to be content with the outdoor temperature.

"Ma'am?" Stacie thought to herself.

"Sorry, Ma'am," the first responder continued. "The road's closed up ahead. We have a tractor-trailer jack-knifed on the Letter S up there. Probably going to be a couple of hours before the road opens up again."

Stacie knew the Letter S was a dangerous curve that claimed about two vehicles a month in the winter. It was an infamous landmark in Higley that warned drivers to slow down and focus on the mountainous road ahead. She had been one of those victims as a teenager when she lost control of her Uncle Ernie's truck and dented the rear fender. Luckily, she was only going 15 miles per hour, which was the posted speed limit. Uncle Ernie never fussed over the dent; even said it gave the old truck character. "Besides," she remembered him saying, "a truck is just a truck. As long as you're okay, then it's nothing to get upset about."

The young first responder stood straight and waved a large tow truck to go around Stacie. The truck's diesel engine groaned and the truck swerved around Stacie's car. The driver behind the wheel stared at the pretty blonde that was forbidden to go forward and then he gave the horn a quick toot as if to say, "Thanks." The young traffic director bent back down to eye level with Stacie again. "You'll have to turn around here, ma'am, and wait until the road is clear."

"Are you sure it's going to be a couple of hours?" Stacie questioned. "Can't that tow truck move it?"

"Naw. Not by himself," He answered. His road flare smile beamed as if he thought Stacie's question was cute. "It'll take a couple of wreckers to move that sonava…um…that truck," he said. His cheeks flushed as he corrected his manners.

"Okay, I'll just come back after the storm has passed. Thank you."

"Drive carefully, ma'am."

Stacie did a three-point turn and headed back to town.

The thought of the Letter S curve and Uncle Ernie gave her the inclination to visit. She could wait at her aunt and uncle's house while the tow trucks removed the ill-fated truck. While she was there, she could fill them in on her little addition to the family. She couldn't wait to tell them because they had been encouraging her and Paul to have a baby for years. Every holiday was a chance to drop little hints about how nice it would be to have a 'little one' in the house. Stacie dreaded those comments. It made her feel pressured to start a family, but now that there would be a baby at family holidays, she looked forward to them.

Back in town, she took a right turn at a little church and navigated the slippery back road that was frosted with three inches of snow. The all-wheel-drive car held its course and brought her to a small hobby farm nestled on top of a hill. The yellow house was built after World War II and had several owners over the years. Ernie Bates bought the house 24 years ago after the previous owner passed away.

From the outside, it wasn't much to look at, and most people would drive by without a second glance. The roof needed to be re-shingled and the paint was fading. The split-rail fence along the front had fallen in a couple of places, and the barn leaned a little to the left. Behind the house, a beautiful meadow sprawled across 16 acres. The meadow was adorned with wild apple trees and rock piles the size of Stacie's car. Enormous oak trees that were seedlings when the Pilgrims arrived grew in each corner of the meadow. An electric fence ran the perimeter of the meadow, keeping Ernie's five horses inside—most of the time.

She pulled into the driveway, scattering a couple of free-range chickens, and parked the car. Her favorite horse, Canyon, stared at her from behind the electric fence. She admired him for a moment; his dark brown coat was contrasting against the snow and a blaze between his eyes that went all the way to his nose. Canyon seemed to be admiring Stacie right back. He remembered her as one of the most gentle souls to ever ride him. She talked to him for a moment in a nearly inaudible voice, but the horse knew what she was saying without understanding the language.

Aunt Marie opened the side door and stood framed by its space. She let Stacie have her moment with Canyon—and let Canyon have his moment with Stacie. She waited at the door wearing an oven-mitt and held their old dog, Alphie, by the collar. The golden colored mutt didn't bark, but he pulled and squirmed to try and make it out the door to greet Stacie. The 58-year-old woman held firm—her strength against Alphie's—and she proved to be the victor.

"Damn, girl. Don't you have the sense to keep off these roads in weather like this?" Aunt Marie admonished.

"Guess not. I think Canyon misses me."

"We all miss you, honey."

132

Aunt Marie noticed Stacie's uniform under her jacket. "Ain't you supposed to be at work?"

"Naw, no flights the rest of the day, so I left early," She gave Aunt Marie a peck on the cheek.

"My good fortune, I guess," smiled Aunt Marie. "How are you, dear? Why in blazes are you out and about in this storm?"

"Well, I wanted to go up to Bear Bay to see Paul. But Route 56 is blocked off by a tractor-trailer accident."

"Oh, I know all about that. Your Uncle Ernie's been up there already checking on it. The truck was leaking a little oil off the side of the road, and he had to file a report saying it wasn't contaminating Cold Brook. He's in his office now, finishing up the paperwork."

Stacie sat in the chair Aunt Marie was gesturing toward and took off her coat. The pellet stove in the kitchen was warm and relaxing as the heat caressed her face. Alphie put his head on Stacie's lap, and Stacie naturally began scratching behind his velvet ears.

"Coffee, dear?" Aunt Marie smiled. She held up a carafe that was half full, proving to Stacie that she didn't have to make a fresh pot.

"Maybe just a little, thanks."

Aunt Marie placed a green coffee cup in front of her brother's daughter and poured too much coffee. Stacie read the little phrase decorating both sides of the cup, "Never give up on what you love." Her index finger followed the handwritten font,

133

and she thought about her baby when she traced the last word. She stirred a little cream and a level teaspoon of sugar into the coffee, then she wrapped her hands around the large cup and relished its warmth. With each sip, she thought about the phrase again, "Never give up on what you love."

Ernie stepped into the kitchen, "Alphie, go lay down." The dog obeyed without hesitation. "Damn girl, what are you doing out this way in weather like this?"

"I asked the same thing," chided Aunt Marie.

Uncle Ernie was in his late fifties. He was broad-shouldered from years of hard work on the farm and stronger than anyone she knew. The only thing that slowed Ernie Bates down was arthritis that was developing in his left hip, which was forcing him to retire in the spring, despite his love for his job. He was an officer with the Department of Environmental Conservation. This spring would mark 31 years working for the state, and he'd stay another 31 if he could. But, Aunt Marie wanted him to slow down a little, and since they were empty-nesters, they wanted to do some traveling.

"I'm going ice fishing, Uncle Ernie," Stacie smirked. "Wanna go?" She stood up and wrapped her arms around his neck.

Ernie joked back, "Last time I went ice fishing, all I caught was hell." He was pointing at Aunt Marie with his thumb.

She snapped a dish towel at him playfully. "That's because you came home at 1:00 in the morning, three-sheets to the wind," Aunt Marie said. "And you didn't have any fish."

The couple chuckled at each other.

Stacie laughed at the two of them. This is what she wanted—to grow old with Paul like Ernie and Marie. She wanted their home to be a happy place where they would raise a family and fill it with memories. She realized how lucky she was and that Higley, NY might not be such a bad place to raise a family. The schools were pretty good, and the neighborhood was safe. The entire community took care of each other, and they had a lot of friends here.

Stacie sat back down at the table. Alphie snuck over and placed his head back on Stacie's lap. She obliged the old dog and recommenced scratching his ears. Stacie explained to them that Paul was still out of work and not having much luck finding a job. The job search and the bills piling up at home were causing him to be depressed. She told them how she encouraged him to go fishing to take his mind off everything at the house. She explained how she was compelled to leave work early to see him, and then she explained why.

"Oh my goodness, you're going to be momma?" Aunt Marie beamed. "You're going to be such a good mother." She hugged Stacie around the neck then finally sat at the table across from her niece. "Oh, and that Paul…he'll be a great dad. He's such a hard worker and a patient man."

Uncle Ernie smiled. "Congratulations, sweetie. 'Bout time we had some little feet running around the house again." Ernie looked at the pictures of there grown children on the kitchen hutch. A few memories of the kids surfaced in his mind, and he reflected on how quiet the house had been for the last four years. All four kids resided in different states now with kids of their own.

"Thanks," Stacie said. "You two are the first to know. I'll have to wait until Paul gets home tonight to tell him."

"You said he's at Bear Bay?" Aunt Marie asked. "Ernie could take you up there on the snowmobile, couldn't you, dear," It was more of an order than a question, but Ernie had no problem with the request.

"Sure, I can take you up. The sled's full of gas and the fresh powder would make for a great ride. Besides, I'd love to see Paul. Can I bring a couple of beers?"

"No, no...I can't impose," Stacie started.

"I insist. We insist," interrupted Aunt Marie. "Besides, you shouldn't be traveling alone today. Haven't you been watching the news?"

"Are you talking about the Canadian that killed the man on the Reservation? I heard all about that. I'm sure that's just some drug deal gone bad, Aunt Marie."

"Well, I hope so, dear. But a pretty young thing like you shouldn't take chances until they catch that bastard."

"Don't worry about her, Marie. She carries a gun."

Stacie shook her head at Aunt Marie but spoke to Ernie. "No, Uncle Ernie, I don't. Just because I'm in security doesn't mean I get a gun."

"We going or not?" Uncle Ernie asked—he was already changing into heavier boots for the cold snowmobile ride. Then he slipped his Carhart bibs over his uniform.

"Yes, yes, go get your beer," Stacie laughed.

The impatient uncle went outdoors to warm up the Yamaha VK 540 snowmobile while Stacie retrieved some warmer clothes from the car. She kept ski pants, mittens, a toque, and boots in a dufflebag because sometimes she met Paul after work to go snowshoeing. She took the bag into the house and layered up for the cool ride ahead. Then she reassured Aunt Marie three times that she would be warm enough. They gave each other another hug and then Stacie jumped on the back of the snowmobile after she argued with Uncle Ernie about who would drive.

The twosome sped across the horse field, only stopping to open the gate on the wire fence, and then accelerated out of sight. Aunt Marie watched from the doorway, holding Alphie by the collar. Once they entered the cedar trees on the far side of the meadow, she let the dog go and headed back into the house. Alphie wimpered on the back porch, watching as if he'd never see the two humans again.

****

Ernie slowed the Yamaha snowmobile as they traversed the cedar trees. The aroma of cedar oil filled Stacie's nose, even through her helmet. They snaked through the woods and made their way to an abandoned road populated by a few hunting camps and summer cottages. The Racquet River flowed parallel to their travels, but the water went north as Ernie and Stacie traveled south. Every few miles, they would ride through a small, frozen river bay, and Stacie would have memories of all the things she and Paul would do on the river—kayaking, swimming, camping, water skiing, hiking, and even geo-caching.

137

Ernie steered the snowmobile to the left, banked the vehicle off the snow, and began up the Gold Mine Trail. The trail was rough and uneven for the first 400 yards as they climbed a steep hill. Once they crested the top, it was smooth and freshly groomed—thanks to the local snowmobile association. The well-groomed trail allowed Ernie to juice the engine some more, and they accelerated to 40 miles per hour. The trail twisted and turned, and as they made their way, they climbed another 400 feet in elevation. The further south they traveled, the lighter the snowfall.

The Gold Mine Trail led them to a logging road that that brought them back toward the river. Six miles down this road, they finally arrived at the intersection of Garrison Road. Ernie locked on the brakes when they approached the green Jeep parked on the side.

He killed the engine and removed his helmet. "Well, I'll be damned."

"What is it?" Stacie asked as her helmet slid off her soft hair.

"This Jeep...I think it's the one that came over the BOLO report this morning," Ernie said. He didn't need to explain to Stacie that 'BOLO' stood for 'Be On the Look Out' since she often received the same reports at the airport.

"Was it related to the Canadian that killed the smuggler on the reservation?"

"I'm not sure, but it appears so. It was reported as stolen, but without the report, I can't verify the license plate number." Ernie stepped off the snowmobile and circled the vehicle, inspecting the tracks in the snow. They were filled in with fresh snow from earlier in the morning, and he decided the vehicle had probably been there all night. Another set of fresh foot prints came out of the woods and went up the road, but Ernie couln't tell if they were made by the same pair of boots.

Stacie reached under her snow-pants and into the pocket of her jeans to retrieve her phone. She thought she could call Daryl at the airport and see if he had received a copy of the BOLO. The phone had no signal, but the message light was blinking. She pulled a mitten off with her teeth and thumbed through to the message. It came through 12 minutes ago—while she and Ernie were traveling on the snowmobile. The noisy engine blocked out the sound of the message chiming when it came through. She read Paul's message and then opened the attached picture.

"Holy shit!" Stacie exclaimed, the words muffled by the mitten she held with her teeth.

"What is it?" Ernie asked.

"This plane…," She removed the mitten. "I think it's the one from the airport this morning."

Ernie looked at the screen, "Hmm, I listened to the scanner all morning. I never heard anything about a plane going down."

"I didn't hear anything about it, either," Stacie agreed. "The pilot would have sent a mayday, don't you think?"

"Not if he was unconscious. Sometimes the stress of flying can cause a heart attack. Or, they could have had mechanical issues or ice build-up when he came through that storm to the north. Was there anyone else on board?"

"Yes, just one."

Ernie shook his head. "That's a shame. Poor guys probably on some business trip thinking they'd be home for dinner with their wives tonight, and then BAM! They're dead."

"I don't think they were on business—legal business, anyway."

"Still a shame. Shitty way to meet your maker."

"Well, it looks like someone from the D.E.C. is there. Look at this picture again," Stacie took her thumb and index finger and placed them on the screen. She spread them quickly to zoom in on the man wearing the state issued uniform. Ernie squinted at the screen, moving it closer to his eyes then further away, struggling to get his old eyes to focus. Finally, he tipped his head back as if he was wearing his reading glasses. His mouth contorted in confusion.

"Ain't got any idea who this fella is," he admitted. "I know every person in the D.E.C., but I've never seen him before. I think we better go check things out—see if they need some help."

Stacie took a closer look at the picture. The man in uniform had a red beard and matched the description on the BOLO she had received and pinned to the bulletin board that morning.

"No way. It can't be. Uncle Ernie, are you sure this guy doesn't work with you?"

"Sure, I'm sure. I'd remember him," Ernie replied.

"I think this could be the guy that killed the smuggler. He fits the description, and it can't be a coincidence that there's a green Jeep sitting here that might be stolen."

140

"Yeah, I think you're right," Ernie said. "I'll bet he stole that Jeep and is posing as an officer. Question is, what is he doing here? What is he after? We need to go warn Paul and his brothers. If this guy is who we think he is, they could be in danger."

"I'm not sure, Uncle Ernie," She slid the phone back in her pocket. "I think we'd better go back to town and report this."

"Sure, we can report a plane has crashed into the river, but do you know who they're going to call to go investigate?"

"You?"

"That's right. I'll have to turn around and drive all the way back up here. So let's go check things out from shore. If it looks like a dangerous situation, we won't approach them, and we'll get our asses out of here."

Stacie pulled the bulky helmet over her head. "Okay, as long as you're sure." She was a little scared of what they might find at the river, but then she convinced herself that she was being paranoid. She tightened the helmet's nylon chinstrap. "Okay, let's get going then."

Ernie climbed on the Yamaha first and turned the key. The engine turned but refused to fire. He tried again, but the result was the same. "Oh come on, you friggin piece of—"

"What's the matter?"

"Not sure. I put fresh gas in it yesterday, and the spark plug is practically new."

Stacie approached the machine and removed her helmet again. A familiar odor filled her nostrils. "Is that gas I smell?"

Ernie raised his visor and lifted the cowl that covered the engine. He, too, could smell the gas and put his face closer to the engine. A few drips caught his attention and then he could see the little hole in the snow where the gas was dripping on the ground. He placed his fingers underneath the engine and waited for a few drips to trickle on to them. Then, he lifted his fingers to his nose and confirmed what they were both fearing. "Yup, that's gas. Looks like there's a crack in the intake line. The engine's sucking air instead of gas."

"Can you fix it?" Stacie asked.

"I was hoping you could."

Stacie looked at him with a "Don't fuck with me" look.

Ernie smiled. "Yes, I can fix it. But not here. I need a new gas line. The crack is right in the middle of the hose, so I can't cut it, or it will be too short."

"What about that Jeep?" Stacie asked. "Think it will make it up the road with all of this snow?"

"Sure it will. Paul drove his truck in further, so this thing oughtta make it." He brushed some of the snow from the top rail and opened the driver's door. He looked above the visor, in the center console, and even on the floor. After a thorough inspection, he determined the keys were gone and broke the news to Stacie.

"Well, it's only about two or three miles to hike it from here. Whatta ya think, kid, feel like walking?"

"Well, it's too far to walk back to your house," Stacie said. She set the helmet on the snowmobile's seat and patted him on the back, "Sorry, Uncle Ernie. I shouldn't have dragged you out here."

"Nonsense, kid, I was just looking for something to do today. Besides, it's too nice a day to be riding that thing anyway. I'd rather be walking. We'll just hitch a ride out of here with Paul."

"What about your hip?"

"Oh, it'll feel better after a half-mile. Walking helps it loosen up. I'll be sore tonight, though, so don't expect me to be out dancin'."

Ernie went to the snowmobile and retrieved the walking stick that was strapped to the foot rail. Then he removed his heavy snow pants that were restricting his movement. Lastly, he went to the back compartment of the snowmobile and lifted out a small cooler with eight Busch beers inside. "Can't celebrate without a few brews, right?"

Stacie left her skipants on but shed her heavy winter coat. She knew she'd be a little chilly as they started out, but by the time they reached Haystack Rock, she'd be sweating. A hair tie was retrieved from her coat pocket and she held it in her teeth while she formed a ponytail in her blonde hair. Then she slid her right hand into the hair tie and transferred it to the ponytail.

They marched south down Garrison Road, following the river and the footprints that were recently made by another person. They knew it had to be the unidentified D.E.C. officer in the photo that made this journey before them. They talked while they walked, trying to piece together the complicated puzzle and figure out the Canadian's motive.

Chapter 14 / *Time to Get Your Ass in the Water*

The Canadian directed Andy to start a fire next to the hole in the ice, so the big man fetched some wood. Once Andy had a satisfied amount of kindle, sticks, and some larger logs, he lit the tinder bundle he had created from a handful of pine needles. The fire climbed the pile of wood as Andy blew into the base. The fire seemed like a hopeful sign to the Marten brothers, who stood at gunpoint waiting for the next move.

Andy had done well not to reveal himself to the Marten brothers, which surprised the Canadian. He never asked Andy to stay incognito, and there was no reason for Andy to keep up the charade. He assumed that once this was over, Andy would stay in Higley and go about his life as if this had never happened. Andy wouldn't want the Marten brothers to know he participated in this crime so he could just go back to a normal life. The money wouldn't change Andy. He was an island in the waves of society; anchored to the ground while the rest of the world flowed around him with big houses, fancy cars, and debts that controlled their lives. Andy would get a share of the money, but he wouldn't change his lifestyle. He loved this area; this town, and the people in it.

The Canadian knew the Martens trusted Andy, but if the truth came out, they might do something radical. For now, they'd keep up the ruse in case they needed to play that card later.

"You go down and get the case," the Canadian addressed the whole group. "I'm sure you saw it on your fish-finder. It's silver and about this big," he held his hands about two feet apart.

"It should be the only thing on the plane. Once I have the case, you get to warm up by the fire. If we don't have any problems, everybody walks away alive. Try something funny, and only I walk away. Understand?"

The Martens said nothing. They wouldn't give the Canadian the satifaction of being scared or nervous and their stoic demeanor was in protest rather than fear.

"Yes, sir," Andy responded.

Paul kneeled on the ice, breaking up some wood while a fire of his own flared inside him. He'd have to risk his life fighting the current while trying not to go into shock from the freezing water. Then he'd have to turn the money over to this asshole. All the ideas he had for the money sank to the bottom of the river to join his ill-fated phone. He thought about ways to get out of the situation and turn the tide on the fake D.E.C. asshole with the pistol. Their options were limited and time was running out. One idea kept running through his mind; if the case was unlocked or open—which it appeared to be since money was floating in the water—then maybe he could stash some in the plane and come back tomorrow to retrieve it.

Andy's fire burned hot now.

"Time to get your ass in the water," the Canadian said while staring down into the dark river.

Paul removed his jacket and started working on his overalls. "Oh no, not you, buddy," The Canadian smiled. "Him," he pointed the gun at Eric, the youngest of the brothers. "I want you right where I can see you," he nodded to Paul.

"He doesn't swim well," Paul cautioned. "Neither of them do. I'm the only strong swimmer here, and with the current in this spot, I'm your best option for success."

"No, you're my back up plan," the Canadian said. "Besides, you're going to be addressing that wound."

"What wound?"

"This one." He swiveled the pistol to Jack and pulled the trigger. The slug from the .357 ripped through Jack's thigh, missing his femur by an inch. Jack whirled 90 degrees and collapsed from the shot. He grabbed his thigh and rolled from side to side in agony. The pain was like a million hot needles were just shoved into his skin at the same time. He wanted the burning to stop, so he grabbed handfuls of snow and began pushing it on the wound. The snow was pooling red as it absorbed the warm blood seeping from the hole.

The Canadian spun the gun on Eric. "Get in the fucking water and get my money, or you're next."

Paul realized the Canadian wasn't going to work with the Marten brothers' strengths, but on their fears. He could see the terror in Eric's eyes as he watched his oldest brother bleed on the ice. Now Paul had a dilemma; big brother is bleeding from a gunshot wound on his left, little brother ready to drown on his right. He knew as bad as Jack's wound was he would survive. "Take a hell of a lot more than that to kill that tough sonavabitch," Paul thought to himself.

Paul made a stop motion with his hand, asking for the Canadian to give them a moment. Paul turned to Eric. "Where's the rope you made?"

Eric pulled the thin line of braided fishing line out of his pocket. Paul snatched it out of his hands, unhooked the straps on Eric's overalls, and wrapped the rope around Eric's chest. While he tied the line, he looked at Jack laying on his back and tried to estimate how much blood he'd lost. He finished the knot and straightened the rest of the line on the ice to release any tangles. He worked as fast as he could, breathing heavy from the exertion and the stress of the situation. Now he needed something heavy to hold the line.

"Andy, take the other end of this line. Don't let go! I need you to help Eric get back up with that case," Paul directed Andy. "Don't pull too hard, just keep a little tension on the line. If the current starts to take him, pull slow and steady—like you've got a 186-pound fish on your hook."

Paul now turned his attention to Jack. He knelt in blood and started peeling back fabric to get a visual of the bullet hole.

Eric slipped off his boots and overalls. He walked in wool socks to the edge of the ice.

Eric hesitated at the edge of the ice. Under his breath, he muttered, "No way this is worth a few million dollars." He looked back to check on Jack and grabbed some mental motivation. His eyes met with the Canadian's. The Canadian knew Eric was still hesitant to enter the water, so he raised the gun, pointing to the back of Paul's head. Eric's heart jumped into his throat, and he felt like he couldn't breathe. Watching Jack's leg burst from the bullet was bad enough, but when he imagined Paul's skull reacting to the bullet with the same destruction, the image was more than he could bear.

Eric stepped off the ice, and the world went black for two and a half seconds.

The 47-degree water was colder than he had imagined. It felt as though the water was squeezing his entire body, like ice and cement were burying him. The sensation was coming from the muscles of his body contracting all at once from the temperature. He opened his eyes and could see better than he expected. This world seemed surreal with the flightless plane parked in an environment more suited for a submarine. The plane was resting at a 40 degree angle with its bent propeller buried in the sand. It tilted a little to the right, supported by the one wing still attached. Fish darted around the plane for protection. Perch, bass, and some river shiners all took refuge around the fuselage and even darted through the open cargo doors to hide within the confines of the Beechcraft.

Eric flipped his body and started pulling at the water with his hands. His descent was slow with all the clothes he was wearing, but he made progress. Then, he seemed to stop as if Andy wasn't giving him any more slack in the line. He turned around and looked up to check the line and realized he had plenty of slack, but the ice above seemed to be moving past him. The ice was not moving, but Eric was. He realized the current had control of him now. He began to panic. His eyes scanned around looking for something to grab. Why couldn't there be a trophy buck frozen in the ice like before? He remembered the look of death in the eye of that deer. He remembered the look of helplessness and fear frozen in time, and it scared the shit out of him—again.

He clawed at the water with open hands, reaching for something that wasn't there. He saw the familiar blackness start to creep into his vision. The rope around his chest pulled taught, removing all slack. He flailed like a caught fish that had just taken the wrong minnow for breakfast. The rope pulled back as the fisherman above the ice reeled in the drowning man. If the rope broke, he'd be swept out toward the main channel of the river. The water was open there, but the distance was too great for anyone to survive underwater that long. Even Paul, the championship swimmer, couldn't make it that far.

"Pull faster, Andy. Pull faster," Eric thought. The rope held intact, keeping Eric from being taken by the mighty Raquette River.

He turned over in the water, belly to the sky so he could look up at the ice. He wasn't sure if he was looking through the gates of Heaven or the hole in the ice that led to the surface—to oxygen. It turned out to be the latter, and the tense rope was pulling him there. Breaking the surface of the water, he gulped for the much-needed oxygen. Fresh air returned to his lungs as Andy stood smiling down at him. The two locked arms by grabbing each other's wrist and Andy lifted the young Marten out of the water as easily as the perch he had hooked earlier that day.

"Hey, buddy, see any fish down there?" Andy asked the waterlogged Eric.

Eric was breathing heavy trying to recover from the ordeal. Panting lungs refused to speak, so Eric just gestured to Andy with his middle finger. The Canadian's head twisted, looking to see if Eric had completed his mission. No case.

"Did you forget why you went down there?" the Canadian asked.

"No, asshole, I didn't forget. The current caught me and started taking me out to the channel."

"Catch your breath, then get back in there."

Eric looked at Paul to see how Jack was doing. Paul was squatting by the fire holding a gaff hook in the hot coals. He'd removed the handle and was heating the straight end until it almost glowed. Then he removed it from the heat and returned to Jack's side. Paul pulled back the material around the wound and snaked the hot metal into the bullet hole with a hiss. The blood vessels began to cauterize, and the bleeding stopped almost completely. Jack grimaced and grunted a little, but wouldn't give the Canadian the satisfaction of hearing him scream. He stared at the Canadian as if to say, "You'll have to do better than this to stop me, motherfucker."

Once Paul removed the hot steel, Jack sat up and then made a motion to stand, but Paul held him down. It took little effort since he couldn't put his weight on the wounded leg. Jack decided to sit a bit and started packing cold snow on the leg again to sooth the burning.

"I've got the bleeding under control," Paul said. "Now let me dive after the money, and then we can all get the hell out of here." He stood and started for the hole in the ice.

"No, youe brother's going to give it one more try,. The words seemed to be coming from the pistol.

"Dammit, he's going to drown!"

The Canadian smirked. "No, no he won't. You see, he's afraid to go down there. I don't know why, but he's not giving it his best effort. Maybe he doesn't care if you all die."

"I'm scared, asshole!" Eric blurted. "Scared to drown. Scared to die. You would be, too, if you'd ever fallen through the ice and almost drowned."

"So, that's it, eh? You've had a bad experience. This isn't your first time under the ice."

"No. Unfortunately, it's not." Eric was kneeling by the fire. His skin flushed red, and it was impossible to determine if it was from anger or if the light from the flame was illuminating his face.

"And why didn't you drown the first time you fell through the ice, Eric?" the Canadian pried.

"Because I got lucky. And, I had them to pull me out," his chin pointed at his brothers.

"And what if your brothers hadn't been there? Do you think you would have found the strength to pull yourself out? You knew your brothers were there—you knew they would save you, didn't you?"

Eric bowed his head for a moment as if to contemplate the Canadian's words. Did he give up the fight? Did he let the river win the battle? How could he have saved himself if the powerful deer couldn't escape the river?

"When a man's scared—really scared—he needs to reach way down deep inside himself. That's where we find strength and determination to succeed—where we find the strength to push ourselves beyond our limits."

The Canadian was looking at the ice, and Paul wasn't sure if he was speaking to them, or to himself.

"Like blowing up planes and stealing money?" Paul retorted.

"Yes! Like blowing up planes, shooting smugglers, and stealing money."

"So, you shot someone else?" Eric inquired. "In the leg, like Jack?"

"No. Not in the leg and not like Jack." He seemed to be truly remorseful, and the Marten brothers were confused by his words.

"That doesn't sound like finding strength to me," Paul retorted. "Sounds like you're a coward. A coward feeding off the strength of others because you don't have the strength to carry your weight."

The Canadian thought about this for a second. "That's one way of looking at it. But, I've carried my own weight all my life. I've worked since I was a teenager to earn everything I have. I trained my ass off to become an operative with the Special Forces. I've studied my brains out to be the best aircraft mechanic in Canada. Every challenge we accept head-on gives us an opportunity to grow and become stronger. The harder the challenge, the deeper you dig until you find what it takes to succeed."

Eric was listening as the fire warmed his body. His hands were stiffening, the first sign of hypothermia. He turned to feel the heat on his back for a moment and then he said to Andy, "I'm ready. I'm ready to go back down."

Andy shot the Canadian a disappointing look. Andy knew his partner had gone too far and that this whole mess was getting out of control. He wanted it to stop. He wanted it all to be over. He just wanted to go back to fishing. "Okay, buddy. If you think you're ready."

****

Eric walked over to the edge of the ice but went to the opposite side he'd entered on his first attempt. "I've got to enter from this side," he said to Andy. "I've got to be on the upside of the current, and then I can grab the plane and pull myself down. When I give the rope two tugs," he demonstrated by pulling the rope twice just to be sure Andy understood, "start pulling. But this time, pull a little faster."

Andy nodded that he understood the directions and checked the line for knots. Then he stood behind Eric and waited for him to plunge. Eric gave Paul and Jack a quick look as if to say, "No problem, I've got this."

Paul watched his little brother while he was applying pressure to Jack's leg. A sense of pride came over him as he watched Eric shed his soaked hoodie. As scared as he was, Eric was risking his life for them. He realized Eric was right—they should have just left and reported the money, no matter how much was in the case. They should have abandoned the ice as soon as the plane crashed. They should have been satisfied with the four fish they had for their freezers. But now, the day had gone to hell, all because of Paul and Jack's greed. Because they had let themselves get into financial trouble, Eric was paying for it dearly; perhaps with his life. Paul knew if anything happened to Eric, he'd never be able to live with the guilt.

Eric's splash disrupted his thoughts.

Below the surface, Eric kept his body as straight as a nail, letting his momentum take him almost to the river's bottom. The current tried to push him away when he reached mid-depth, but he was moving fast this time. Eric's feet hit the top of the plane above the single engine. He jumped into a squat position and grabbed the plane. There was little to hang on to since the plane's aerodynamics forbid anything protruding from its profile. Eric's hands and feet slipped against the slick metallic surface, and he hustled to find something to hold. The broken window on the copilot side offered a handhold. Broken glass tore at the flesh of his palm, but his grip stayed true.

The silver case was lying on the floor of the plane, but the window had too many shards of glass to reach through. The window looked like the mouth of a giant shark with dagger-like teeth ready to tear him open and swallow him from the world. Then Eric realized that the window was part of a door; a door into the cockpit. He twisted the handle and pulled to gain access, but the door would barely budge. The impact of the crash had bent and twisted the plane's frame, jamming the door shut permanently.

There was no time to think about his next move. He needed to get inside the plane as soon as possible. He pointed his hands toward the open cargo doors and pushed off the wing with his legs. The effort sent him gliding through the doors and into the body of the wreckage.

The interior of the plane sheltered him from the everlasting current. His heart was racing, but, closer to his goal, he relaxed a little. He pulled, rather than swam, his way down to the cockpit of the Beechcraft. His lungs started to tighten a little, wanting to exhale the carbon dioxide building inside. He fought the urge. Ozzy Sullivan's dead body lay horizontally across the controls of the cockpit, and the only way for Eric to access the case on the floor was to move him.

Time and oxygen were running out.

Eric finally positioned Ozzy's body out of his path and dove down to the case which was open and losing some of the loose bills inside. Most of the money was bundled, but a few of the bundles had broken open during the crash or perhaps the explosion. Eric closed the case to avoid losing the rest of the money on the way up and rolled the tumblers on the combination lock. He wondered if the Canadian knew the combination—then again, that wasn't his problem.

The case was light underwater, and as Eric swam back through the plane, he stopped at the cargo doors. He grabbed the rope around his chest and gave it two tugs. Then he kicked off from the planes wooden floor, out through the cargo doors, and into the current. The force of the current pressed against his clothes but then he felt a greater force pull. Andy's silhouette, standing on the ice, was pulling the young Marten brother to safety. The current attempted to prevent Eric's escape from the river, but Andy would not be denied his prize catch. Eric floated upward and his head popped above the surface. He let out an audible gasp and then breathed a great sigh of relief and fresh Adirondack air. He clung to the ice with his left arm; elbow bent with his chin on his forearm. He then brought his right arm into view and handed the coveted case to Andy. Andy ignored the case and went straight to Eric's left hand. The big man dragged Eric onto the ice for the second time today.

Paul ran to his brother's side. "Are you okay?"

"Yeah, yeah, I'm fine," Eric conceded. He was standing, but bent over with his hands on his knees trying to catch his breath. "I'm in a lot better shape than the pilot."

The Canadian's head sunk for a moment at the thought of Ozzy being down there. He'd been so focused on the money that he'd forgotten about the fate of the Irishman. He was glad his eyes did not have to be tortured by the sight of a man, once so full of life, rotting away at the bottom of the river. Ozzy's life was thrown away, but the Canadian convinced himself that it was a necessary sacrifice that would be worth it in the end.

"See?" the Canadian boomed. "You dug deep, son. I knew you had it in you to get the job done." He was smiling for the first time since arriving on the ice. The Canadian lifted the case from the ice and went back to the seat he had taken from Andy.

"It's locked," Eric said. "I had to shut it and lock it to get it up here, or the money would be on its way to the St. Lawrence River."

"That's okay, kid. Skiff's not the sharpest hook in the water. He uses the same combination for all his locks." He rolled the tumblers a few times, and with a click, the case popped open. "See? 1966—that's the year of his classic Ford Mustang."

The Canadian seemed satisfied with what he saw inside. He reached in and grabbed four bundles of cash and threw them on the ice. "Here, fellas—you earned it."

Each bundle was almost a half-inch thick. Each bill was worth $100 , and Paul estimated there were 100 bills per bundle—

10 thousand dollars in each bundle. The temptation to pick up one of the bundles knawed at his wallet. He didn't know if they could trust the Canadian and his promise that they would just walk away, but this gesture was encouraging.

"So now what?" Paul dared. "We all just go our separate ways and pretend this never happened?"

"That's right. You didn't see me, and I never saw you. I know you're all local boys, so if I have to, I'll come to find you."

Paul remembered the fake D.E.C. officer asking for their fishing licenses and identifications. He knew their names and addresses, so he probably wasn't bluffing.

"Where'd the money come from?" Eric asked. "At least let us know who we helped you rip off."

The Canadian considered the question. He pulled Andy's chair a little closer to the fire and sat back down. His knees supported his forearms, and he talked as if he were speaking to his SIG 226. "The money came from my arms dealing, drug smuggling, scum of the Earth boss. I'm not stealing from the church or a school, and nobody's going to be missing their inheritance. A few mafia bosses and some gang-bangers are going to be pissed, but not at me. By the time they figure out it was me, I'll be in Mexico. I've got connections, too, and can disappear there. You guys…," he waved the gun back and forth, "…will never see me again." Then he stepped up to the fire to absorb a little more of the addictive heat.

Paul helped Jack stand and walked him to the fire. He needed to give Eric a chance to heat up before they made the trek to Andy's cabin. With a four-feet long stick, he poked the fire to give the hot coals fresh oxygen. The flames danced with energy now, and the coals glowed back to life. Paul and Andy piled sticks and logs of spruce, maple, and hemlock to satisfy the hungry fire. The Canadian picked up the folding chair he'd been using and set it on the ice behind Jack and then gestured for him to have a seat. "Better stay off the leg for a while, eh?"

"Don't you have somewhere you need to be?" Jack snarled. He was pale and weaker than usual, but his spirit wouldn't break. He hesitantly took the seat and groaned a little on the way down. Jack sat with his wounded leg straight out in front of him and lit another cigarette.

While they warmed by the fire, the 40 thousand dollars the Canadian had dropped for them lay on the ice. No one looked at it. No one picked it up. No one talked about it.

Chapter 15 / *Haystack Rock*

Stacie and Ernie heard the distant gunshot, which split the air like thunder. The Canadian had fired the pistol by Paul's feet, threatening the Martens to go after his money. The snow on the trees muffled the sound as it echoed off the ridges, making it difficult to discern where it originated. Ernie held his breath to listen intently for a second shot, but it never came.

"Do you think that came from the river?" Stacie asked her uncle.

"Hmm. Hard to say. Could be someone rabbit hunting up this way, but that sounded like a pistol to me." The old man had a keen sense of hearing because he always wore ear protection when working with machinery on the farm. He even wore hearing protection when he vacuumed in the woodworking shop. Stacie used to tease him that he only wore earplugs so he couldn't hear Aunt Marie yelling at him. It was partially true. "Com'on, we've got about a mile to go."

"How's your hip doing?"

"Great. I'll be sore tomorrow, but it feels pretty good right now. Hey, look. There's Paul's truck."

Paul's truck was parked off the road in a little clearing some hunters created to unload ATV's and meet for a weekend outing. The clearing was about the size of a house and surrounded by thick evergreens. To the right of the clearing, a short wall built from railroad ties held an embankment of dirt to form a loading ramp. Hunters and outdoorsmen could back their trucks up to the ramp and unload their all-terrain vehicles. Ernie walked around the truck, just to inspect for any vandalism.

The footprints around the truck were snowed in now and barely visible. It was apparent, though, that three men had exited the truck, retrieved gear from the bed, and then dragged their sleds up Garrison Road for 100 yards.

The sight of Paul's truck brought a smile to Stacie's lips because she felt like he was just around the corner from her.

Stacie and Ernie marched the length of a football field down the road and then turned right at Haystack Rock—a famous landmark for hunters, campers, and berry pickers, that stood 15 feet high. The rock, composed of solid granite with a ribbon of quartz, had been deposited here eons ago by a glacier. It was hard to say where it came from, but now it was an anomaly making its home in the Adirondack forest. The pinkish-brown boulder was surrounded by thick evergreens with its hardened surface contrasting against the softness of the pine needles. White snow covered one side of Haystack Rock and the dark green pine limbs with their share of snow made for a beautiful scene.

Stacie stopped to capture the placid scene on her phone camera, hoping it would look as good on screen as it did in real life.

"Why don't you rest for a minute," Stacie offered.

"Maybe a minute. I don't want to take too long to get to the river."

Ernie took a seat on a tree stump, conscious to stay out of Stacie's pictures. He watched her hold the phone out, push the

161

shutter button several times and smile at the results. He adored Stacie and her love of nature. She used to photograph all the beauty of the area when she was younger but ended up selling her camera to help pay her parents debts. Ernie didn't know she sold her camera, or that she'd taken over her parents debt, but he always knew there was something she wasn't telling him. He thought about the six framed pictures that adorned the walls of his home. Beautiful shots of waterfalls, flowers, and old barns that every guest admired when they visited. Ernie was fond of the pictures because they were memories of their hikes together. Almost all of those photographs were taken with Ernie standing somewhere behind Stacie. He cherished those memories when Stacie spent summers with him and Aunt Marie, and his hip allowed him to be more active.

"Why don't you take pictures anymore?" Ernie asked. He laid his walking stick across his lap and set the little cooler of beer on the ground.

"Sold my camera," her face saddened a little. She forgot how much she loved photography. "We just haven't had the money to replace it. Now that Paul and I have a baby on the way, I may have to wait a few more years to buy one."

"Having a baby is the perfect time to buy a camera. There's going to be a lot of 'Kodak moments' over the next few years you'll want to capture—first baths, first sitting up, crawling, walking. Before you know it, you'll be taking pictures of her first car, prom, and graduation."

"I know, but until Paul goes back to work, we're living on a shoestring budget."

Ernie saw it was a sore subject and chose not to pry. He made a mental note about the camera and what he'd get her as a baby-shower gift. Aunt Marie would know where to buy the best camera.

Ernie pulled a flask out of the inside pocket of his jacket. He unscrewed the top and sipped the liquid contents. Smooth brandy coated his throat and warmed him from the inside out.

"Uncle Ernie, where did you get that?" Stacie asked when she saw the shiny flask.

He took another sip, wiped his mouth with the back of his hand, and tucked the flask back into the pocket from where it came. "Little something to keep me warm on a day like this."

"It's 30 degrees out. It's not that cold."

"Cold enough," Ernie smiled. Then his eyes focused past Stacie and through the branches of the snow-covered pines. He rose to his feet and walked off the trail without his walking stick or cooler. Twenty yards into the woods, he studied the ground. There was some debris scattered around the floor of the woods—white and red pieces of metal mixed in with freshly broken tree limbs. "Would you look at that?"

Stacie thought he stepped off the trail to relieve himself and didn't dare to turn around. "What is it?"

"Looks like pieces of that plane, I'd say. It must've gone through these treetops before crashing into the river."

Stacie walked over and stood by his side.

"Hmm," he said looking at the ground. "These footprints are fresh. Someone's been walking around these pines. Looks like a big fella by the boot."

"Who do you think it could've been? That D.E.C. officer in Paul's photo?"

"Those are my tracks," a strange voice said from the woods.

Stacie jumped and grabbed Ernie's arm. A shadowy figure emerged through some evergreen boughs and stood just 20 yards away. Mason Blankenship had survived the crash, although he was never really in it. Once the wounded Beechcraft airplane started skimming the treetops and slowing down, he jumped through the plane's cargo doors into the thick canopy of green needles. Blood covered half of his head. His left eye was swollen black, and his left ear had a large tear in it. The kevlar vest he was wearing prevented his vital organs from being impaled by tree limbs, but not from cracking a few ribs. The fall from the trees caused a lot of bruising and scratches, and he lost consciousness for 45 minutes, nearly freezing to death before he finally awoke and built a fire.

The explosion from Cordelia's blast had little effect on the big man. Most of the ball-bearings projected at the plane had missed him. One ball-bearing went through his right calf muscle, and two hit him in the right forearm. Of the two that hit his arm, one lodged into his ulna, and the second just grazed some skin and fat.

The large bodyguard had been walking the woods looking for his prized HK-416. Once he located the weapon, he scoured the woods trying to determine which direction the plane had traveled.

It was difficult for him to discern after becoming disoriented from his tumble through the tree boughs. Blankenship was a stranger here, and the trees kept the secret of the plane's location to themselves. The plane had shred some of the treetops, causing pine needles and splinters of wood to litter the snow on the ground. The winter sky was overcast, so discerning north from the south was difficult for a man who'd just been dropped from the sky. He intended to find the wreckage and recover the money Skiff hired him to protect, but after everything he'd been through, he had no intentions of returning the money. Now, he wanted possesion of the case and the three million dollars locked inside.

Lucky to be alive, he felt he had a chance to disappear with the money—if the case survived the crash. He'd hitch-hike his way west and meet up with an old friend in Minnesota. That would keep him close to the Canadian border, in case he ever needed to flee the U.S. Blankenship was tired of being Skiff's pawn, taking risks and breaking laws was getting tiresome. He barely survived this time, and it was just a matter of time before his luck ran out. Maybe he'd meet a nice girl in Minnesota and settle down.

He laughed at the thought. Screw that! Skiff would think he was dead so he was a free man now. There was no way he'd let someone else tie him down. He was going to take that money and build his own empire. Drugs, guns, stolen cars, and women—that was more his style.

"Who the heck are you?" Stacie asked in a voice as soft as a chickadee's. She did not want to spook the battered stranger.

Blankenship skirted the question. "I was on that plane you're talking about. We were sabotaged in-flight by a bomb. The pilot was killed instantly and the left wing was almost blown clean off. I knew it was going to be a hard landing so I bailed. I saw the pines under us and figured that would be a softer landing."

"Looks like you were right, or maybe just lucky," Ernie observed. "Where'd you guys come from? The plane, I mean. Where the heck did you fly out?"

"Burlington," Blankenship answered. He approached the D.E.C. officer and his niece.

"Vermont?" Ernie asked.

"Yeah, we were headed to Syracuse. Business trip, you know."

Stacie knew the big man was lying. She knew that the plane came out of Canada and had stopped at her airport just hours ago for mandatory international inspection. That was when she saw Greene take the bribe money. This man standing before her must have been inside the plane during the inspection. Stacie saw the assault rifle on the sling that was over his shoulder and didn't dare challenge Blankenship's story. She and Uncle Ernie needed to move on—now.

"Who the hell would want to take down your plane?" Ernie asked in confusion.

"Hard to say, sir, but I think it must have been a disgruntled mechanic. He's the only one who had access to the plane in the last 48 hours."

Blankenship had never seen the cause of Ozzy's horror. He never saw Cordelia flying straight at them with her malevolent intentions. He assumed the blast came from the inside of the

Beechcraft. The only thing he knew for sure was who was to blame.

"Well, it looks like you need to get some medical attention, fella," Ernie said.

"I'm fine. I need to find that plane first. There are some important…documents… that I need to retrieve. Then I'll get medical attention, eh?"

"What's with the HK, son? Looks like it was a pretty serious business trip," Ernie said.

"You know your guns. Law Enforcement?"

Ernie pulled back his jacket carefully, trying not to spook the crash survivor. He revealed the badge on his belt. "Environmental Conservation Officer. I'm not trying to be nosey, but it's my job to ask you about that rifle. It's not legal in this state."

"Well, I'm the bodyguard for a senator, so I have a special permit. We were on our way to pick him up."

More lies.

"Sure, sure," Ernie said. "May I see your 'permit?'"

"That's one of the documents I need from that plane. Hopefully, my briefcase survived the wreck."

Stacie took a step back and thought to herself, "Oh no, Uncle Ernie. Stop talking. Stop talking. This man looks crazy." She didn't dare speak the words. She could see Ernie's demeanor change from fun-loving uncle to keen-eyed cop.

"I'm going to ask you for some identification. I'm also going to ask that you remove the magazine from that HK and hand it to me. You see, we have a law in New York that no firearm can hold more than seven rounds. I'm guessing that's a 20 round magazine, right?"

"You want my gun?" Blankenship asked.

"No, No. You can carry the gun empty. I just want the magazine and the round in the chamber."

"Sorry, old man, you're not taking my magazine or my gun." Blankenship's voice went gruff.

Ernie took offense to the term 'old man,' and could feel the heat building under his collar. He didn't feel old, other than an athritic hip, and he sure the hell wasn't going to let some hot-head with a gun insult him.

"Well if you don't comply, you'll be charged with disobeying an officer," Ernie admonished. "You don't want that. All you need to do is hand me the magazine. We'll go find this plane you're looking for, and get everything straightened out."

"I don't think you know who you're dealing with, gramps," Blankenship guffed. "I think you and your lady friend should turn around and go back the other way."

"This is the last time I'm going to ask."

Stacie's heart was pounding. Sweat beaded on her forehead and her stomach felt like a Rubik's Cube twisting and spinning inside her. She suppressed the contents of her stomach from reappearing, but it took all her concentration. The situation was getting out of control. This man had been through enough, but Stacie and Ernie both knew his story was full of holes.

"Listen," Ernie said, "I don't want any trouble here. My pregnant niece is with me, and I'm not taking any chances of anything harming her."

Blankenship turned in the direction the plane had flown, ignoring Ernie. He reached down and grabbed fresh snow and placed it into his mouth. He was thirsty, and the lack of blood muddled his reasoning. Blankenship had never been in a situation like this—a tiny woman and an old man threatening him. He was supposed to be the intimidating one. He was the tough guy. He was the professional killer. It was time to take over the situation.

Ernie took one step closer. He wanted to be close enough to react if Blankenship got stupid. Then, Blankenship got stupid.

Blankenship racked the bolt on the HK with his right hand and spun toward Ernie. Ernie did not see it eject a bullet, which meant he was racking a bullet into the chamber. The gun was pointed 45 degrees toward the ground as he spun around. Ernie's powerful grip snatched the 16-inch gun barrel and held it like a vice. Five flashes of light appeared from the muzzle of the gun as Blankenship pulled the trigger on the fully automatic HK-417. Every bullet that exited the gun barrel hit the snowy ground behind Ernie, who was watching Stacie and keeping the gun pointed away from her.

Stacie stepped backward, tripped on a log and fell to her ass. The fresh snow cushioned her fall, and she was unharmed. She propped herself up on her elbows and watched the scuffle in horror.

Ernie maintained his grip on the gun barrel with his left hand. His right hand grabbed Blankenship by the collar and pushed him backwards until he pinned him against a large pine tree. Blankenship brought his left elbow around, striking Ernie in the right cheek. The blow should have dropped Ernie to his knees, but the seasoned farmer had spent a lifetime kicked by horses, rammed by goats, and hit by bulls—Blankenship's elbow seemed weak in comparison and did not affect the white-haired officer. Blankenship kept the barrage of elbows coming. Ernie kept slamming Blankenship against the tree. The trade of blows caused the tree to shake from the bottom to the top. The branches released a white cascade of fresh snow. For a few moments, the altercation was invisible to Stacie. She wanted to scream, but the sound was stuck in her lungs.

Blankenship realized he underestimated the older man. He'd fought bikers, professional boxers, and other bodyguards before. He thought this would be one more man he'd send to the ground bleeding, but Ernie had been hardened by years on a farm from carrying water pails, throwing hay bales, and chopping wood. His power was impressive for a man of any age. Blankenship's elbows were getting slower and weaker, while Ernie's strength endured. Ernie finally released Blankenship's collar and threw a few roundhouses himself. His police training had taken over, and he went from defense to offense. His left-hand never relinquished its grip on the HK—he had to keep it pointed in a safe direction—but the right arm was free to fight.

The pine tree shook loose the last of its blinding snow and Stacie could see the melee fully. She'd never seen Uncle Ernie in any situation like this. The sweet man she knew was full of fire and fury and in the fight for his life. She made her way to her knees and looked for a stick or rock, anything to help her uncle—there was nothing.

Ernie yanked the big bodyguard away from the tree. Fresh blood began to flow over the dried blood on Blankenship's face. Ernie lifted the HK-416 above Blankenship's head which gave him the opportunity to step through with his right leg and plant his right foot behind Blankenship's right leg. He then thrust his palm into Blankenship's chest, sweeping the bodyguard off his feet and onto his back. The HK let loose from Blankenship's shoulder, and Ernie tossed it into the snow. Now, the weapon was out of the equation, and Ernie had the upper hand.

Blankenship still had some fight left in him. He rolled to his left away from Ernie, but the D.E.C. officer kept coming. This time, Ernie grabbed the sides of Blankenship's kevlar vest at the shoulders. Blankenship tried swinging in desperation with left, right, left, combination punches, but Ernie's elbows blocked each attempt. Blankenship's last resort was to utilize his knees. He brought the right knee up into Ernie's ribs, and for the first time during the brawl, Ernie felt some pain.

Blankenship could sense that Ernie kept his weight on his right leg, obviously favoring a weak left knee or hip. He kept the knees coming at Ernie's left side trying to take advantage of the weakness. Finally, on the forth blow, Ernie timed the knee-strike perfectly and caught Blankenship's right knee under his arm. Now on one leg, Blankenship was vulnerable to Ernie's leg sweep again. Ernie stepped through and placed his right leg behind Blankenship's left leg and gave him another blow to the heart. The impact could have knocked down a tree, but the bullet proof vest absorbed the force. The powerful blow sent Blankenship backward, but not before he could retrieve the semi-automatic .22

caliber pistol from the ankle holster strapped to the trapped leg. As he fell, Blankenship flipped the safety and squeezed off three shots.

Stacie's scream finally broke loose, which was louder than the *pop, pop, pop,* of the small pistol.

Ernie felt the impact of the lightweight bullet slam his chest. The second bullet grazed the base of his neck and shoulder. As he fell back and to the left, the third bullet caught him in the skull, just above and behind his right ear. When he landed, his head struck the log that had tripped Stacie. He lay motionless half buried in the snow. Stacie jumped to his side and gave him a little shake. Tear's flooded her eyes and dripped from her cheeks into the snow.

"No, no, no, no, no," she pleaded. "Uncle Ernie, please wake up! Don't leave me here, please."

She grabbed his hand to comfort them both. She felt a little squeeze from her uncle's hand and then the pressure faded. She was ready to stay there all day to be with her beloved uncle in his last moments on Earth, but a sinister shadow lingered over her ominously. She felt a powerful grip snag her by the collar and Blankenship was pulling her to her feet.

"Get your sweet ass up, honey," Blankenship ordered. "He's dead. If you don't want to be next, then show me how to get to the plane wreck. I know you know these woods, so get moving." He gestured with the pistol for her to move and then reacquired his assault rifle. Stacie couldn't take her eyes off Uncle Ernie. Blankenship pulled her by the arm in one direction while she kept her eyes on Ernie looking for one more glimpse of life. One more chance to make eye contact. One more little smile from a man who'd given her so much in life.

All she saw instead, was the red stain in the snow growing larger with each passing second.

Blankenship turned Stacie around and stared straight into her eyes. "Find that plane, and you and your baby get to go home tonight." He was pointing the gun at her abdomen. Stacie was horrified by the thought of what this sick killer would do if she didn't comply. She took a deep breath to compose herself, to regain her dignity, and to do what was necessary to survive. One way or another, this baby was going to be raised by her mother.

Blankenship followed Stacie through the woods, matching her steps in perfect rhythm. They weaved through the tall pines with the sun behind them. It must have been lunch time because her stomach growled with dissatisfaction. Even though her pregnant body craved nourishment, food was the last thing on her mind. Her steps were slow, and her boots and heart were heavy. She deliberately set a slow pace and meandered through the trees to lengthen their journey.

The twosome stepped over a small creek which exited into the Raquette River, and Stacie remembered her and Paul camping there years ago. They had kayaked to the area, pitched a tent, and spent three wonderful days under the stars with no distractions; no TV, no phones, and almost no clothes. They skinny dipped where the creek melded into the river, very much like their bodies had during that same swim. Paul caught fish while Stacie peeled potatoes and they made simple dinners over an open campfire that would put most restaurant food to shame. When they kayaked away from their campsite, Paul promised they'd come back every year. That was three years ago.

What happened? Why had life gotten so crazy-complicated? How did they lose control of their schedules? Three years ago, all they had was a tent, a couple of kayaks, and some fishing poles. It was the happiest they had ever been. Not that they weren't happy now, but there were so many distractions in their lives that it watered down the very experience of life itself. They were distracted by their phones, computers, and chores. They were distracted by their volunteer work, their friend's events, and family issues. They were distracted by work, side jobs, hobbies, and online courses.

She missed those days of simplicity and quietness. Now they were bringing a baby into the world—their world. How were they going to make time for a baby when they barely made time for each other? She was scared. Would this baby come between them or bring them back to those days when all they had was each other?

The hiking had caused her to break a sweat. She unzipped her down vest. A gentle wind came across the river and cooled her face. The pines around her seemed to whisper, but she couldn't make out the words. After a quarter-mile, she stopped abruptly.

"We're here," she said to Blankenship. Her voice cracked as she spoke the words. She pointed through an opening in the evergreens to five men standing around the tail of the wrecked plane that protruded from the frozen river. In that group, she recognized the stance of her husband. She'd hoped he would be gone by the time they arrived—on his way home with his fresh catch and a satisfying smile.

"Good girl," Blankenship said. Stacie wanted to knock the smug smile off his face.

"No one else needs to get hurt. Just get your stupid documents and leave. These guys are locals that mean you no harm. You've already killed my uncle; please don't kill my..." she trailed off.

"Your husband?" Blankenship grinned. "I heard your whole conversation with your uncle. I know one of these guys is your husband."

Stacie could see Blankenship's grip tighten around the assault rifle as he watched the five men standing around the fire. "What are you going to do?"

He was silent for a moment, then said, "Whatever I have to."

"Let me talk to them first. I can get them all to leave if you give me a chance. You won't have any confrontation if they leave."

"No, you keep your mouth shut. Besides, you're going to have a gun pointed at your head."

Stacie's heart was racing. Thoughts began to jumble in her mind like popcorn popping. She saw images of the men lying in the snow bleeding. She envisioned Paul taking his last breath as he held her hand. She worried he would end up like Ernie. She couldn't let that happen.

A tree branch lay on the ground next to her—an opportunity. She grabbed the dead branch as Blankenship stared beyond the pines to the icy scenario. She swung the branch at his

175

head with every ounce of power she could muster. The limb was more corroded than she expected; it smashed on impact and Blankenship merely stumbled a little. Without thinking, he instinctively spun around with the butt of the rifle and cracked Stacie in the head. She had turned her skull just before impact, causing her head to whip to the left violently. She felt her body dropping but only saw flashes of light and then darkness.

Stacie lay in the snow unconscious. Blankenship knew he couldn't use her as a hostage and he didn't have time to wait until she woke. Now, he'd have to do this the hard way.

Chapter 16 / *Come and Get It*

Again, Eric's keen eyes caught the movement in the woods. "Someone's over there."

The Canadian didn't turn around. He checked his pistol to be sure the safety was off and watched for a reaction from the brothers and Andy to determine if the new arrival was a threat.

The fire was beginning to die down, and Eric's hypothermia was causing him to tremble. Jack's adrenaline and endorphins had worn off, and the pain from the gunshot was getting worse. Paul wasn't sure which brother he was more worried about, but it was imperative that they both get to Andy's cabin within the next 20 minutes. Andy left a fire going before he set out for the day and ensured Paul that he had some medical supplies for Jack's leg—plus the Jim Beam.

"We need to get out of here," Paul said to everyone. As he said the words, the man in the shadows of the pines stepped into clear view. He was still 200 yards away, but Paul could see he was a big man. The new arrival wore dark clothes that didn't appear to be a uniform or appropriate winter apparel. He was tall and broad-shouldered, although his legs were thin as stilts. The Canadian still kept his focus on the fire, not wanting to reveal himself to whoever was approaching from behind.

Though his eyes were open, the Canadian's mind was elsewhere. He was standing on the green grass looking down at that same tombstone that had been haunting him for days. The flowers were different this time—taller, brighter, and whispered an inaudible sound to him. Then ice began to form over the granite and blood trickled from the sweet flowers. The hummingbird returned to sip the sweet nectar but hummed angrily at all the blood.

"Is he carrying a gun?" Jack asked.

The Canadian's attention snapped back to reality. "Eh?" He turned around slowly. Blankenship was now 75 yards away and stopped right in the middle of his step when he recognized the Canadian mechanic. The Canadian recognized Blankenship, too. The two stared at each other for a moment. The three brothers looked at each other in confusion and assumed the Canadian's partner had just shown up.

"You sonovabitch!" Blankenship yelled. "I knew you were behind this!"

"Blankenship, you lucky asshole," the Canadian swore. "I should have put a bullet in you before this plane left."

The brothers were more confused than ever. The Canadian turned his head but kept his eyes on Blankenship. "Boys, you best head to Andy's cabin now. Shit's about to get real. I'm keeping my promise to let you go. When I'm done killing the hell out of this bastard, I'll be on my way, too."

Paul threw Eric's jacket to him so he could put it on. Andy helped Jack stand up, and they all started walking toward shore as fast as they could. They knew they needed to hurry. As crazy as the Canadian seemed, the new man on the scene may be even crazier, especially based on the way he looked.

"What's the matter, fellas?" Blankenship shouted. "Don't you want to stay for the party?"

"Leave them outta this, eh?" the Canadian grunted. "This is between you and me, Blankenship."

The afternoon sun was reflecting off the silver case and clearly in Blankenship's view. It satisfied him to see the case was not in the plane, and saved him the trouble of diving after it.

"Drop my money and go with your friends and I'll consider saving the ammo," Blankenship offered.

"You want it, come and get it," the Canadian snarled.

"You know how this is going to end, so why don't you do yourself a favor? I'm leaving here with that money or neither of us is leaving."

"I promise, Blankenship, you're not leaving this bay alive."

"Better men than you have tried to kill me."

The Canadian was a former Special Forces officer with the Canadian military. Trained to be one of the most elite soldiers in the country, he could easily take Blankenship in hand-to-hand combat. However, this was not hand-to-hand combat, and Blankenship's gun was better suited for mid-range shooting. The Canadian could see Blankenship's face was bloody and the way he kept his elbows close to his body indicated his ribs were badly bruised or broken, which would affect his aim. If he could keep moving, he should be able to out-shoot the bodyguard. He needed Blankenship to keep shooting, too, and more importantly, keep missing so he'd exhaust all his ammunition. Once Blankenship ran out of bullets, the Canadian could move in and finish the fight with his SOG military knife.

Blankenship noticed the pistol was the only weapon in the Canadian's possession. Sure, he probably had his SOG, with the five-inch blade, sheathed in his belt, but he'd never be close enough to use it. He knew his years of martial arts training and physical size could overpower the Canadian if this were hand-to-hand combat. However, this was not hand-to-hand combat. The Canadian's gun was more suited for close range, so Blankenship needed to keep some distance between them. If he could keep moving, the Canadian would soon run out of ammunition. Then, he could move in and finish him with the .22 caliber pistol strapped to his ankle.

Paul, Eric, Jack, and Andy were on the shore as the stand-off continued. They left their fishing gear behind, along with four northern pikes they had caught that morning.

"Those assholes are going to kill each other," Andy said. He seemed worried.

"Who cares?" Paul responded. "Let 'em, and then we'll get the money."

"Jesus, Paul, there's already one person dead down there," Eric said. "Don't you think that's enough? You act like you'd kill both of those men if you had a gun."

"I just might," Paul said. They kept walking and wouldn't make eye contact as they argued.

"You're telling me that money's worth taking a man's life?"

"No, but these assholes brought this on. All I wanted was to spend the day fishing with you and Jack. I didn't ask for this shit. I didn't expect something like this to happen."

"None of us did, but it's happening, and we're going to get ourselves killed." Eric stopped and looked back at Jack. "How are we going to explain all of this when we get out of here?"

Paul stopped, too, and waited for Jack and Andy to catch up. "We tell the truth. We'll leave out the part about the money."

"Let's keep moving," Jack suggested. Paul could sense his anxiety and knew he must be in excruciating pain. If Blankenship killed the Canadian, he'd probably come after them. Following their tracks in the snow would be easy, and he'd have no trouble catching up. Paul couldn't believe it, but he was rooting for the fake D.E.C. officer who almost killed his brothers to win this fight. He had let them go; kept his word and seemed like he'd disappear now. The newest stranger to arrive seemed dangerous and unpredictable.

Paul peered through the trees and down to the ice. They had put 100 yards between themselves and the two men circling each other. Paul watched the case in the Canadian's left hand. He reflected for a moment on the things he could buy and do with that money. He remembered the overdue bills waiting for him at home and thought about Stacie having to leave for work at 4:30 every morning. Why did she keep doing that? Because she felt she had to; because she felt obligated. The answer to all their financial problems was right there in front of him, but now he needed to walk away, keep from getting shot, and tend to his brothers. He turned away from the bay and, unknowingly, away from his unconcious wife.

They climbed another 15 yards and crested the hill. Now, they were out of sight. As the foursome reached the top, they could see Garrison Road winding through the trees. The road curved around the bay, copying the river's shape almost perfectly. In the late 1800s, it was a horse and wagon trail that loggers used to haul pulp-wood from the area. Now, it was an access road for the power company and hunters. The only maintenance it received was from the hunting clubs and Andy, who was the only person to reside here year-round.

"It will be a lot easier walking once we hit the road," Andy offered. "Almost there."

Jack's leg was bleeding again, and Eric could feel his wet clothes stiffen from the freezing temperature. They had to keep moving and get to Andy's warm cabin as fast as they could. They weaved through the hemlocks, the smell of pine drifting on the wind until they were almost to the road. The road ran through the hardwood trees, which gave an open view of the forest. Somewhere nearby, a pileated woodpecker chipped away at a dead tree. Other than their boots scuffing the ground, it was the only sound they could hear.

Once they were on the road, the drumming of the woodpecker was replaced by the sound of gunfire from the river. The sound was muffled by the fluffy whiteness that surrounded them, clinging to every tree branch, rock, and stick. It was like being inside a giant sound studio with bright lights and no door.

Paul felt some relief when he heard the shots ring out. He envisioned both men shooting each other to death and laying dead on the ice with no one to care except the crows that would come to feed on their carcasses. He would sneak down after the blood stopped oozing from the bullet holes in their torso's and claim the case of money for himself, Stacie, and his brothers. He wouldn't know the outcome of the duel unless he came back later to investigate the scene. He checked the position of the sun and guessed it was around 1:30 in the afternoon, so that gave him plenty of time to return before dark.

Chapter 17 / *Stand Off*

Both Blankenship and the Canadian circled clockwise, sizing each other up and thinking about each other's weaknesses. The Canadian began sprinting as fast as he could while trying to maintain traction on the snow-covered ice. Blankenship mimicked the older man's move by sprinting as fast as he could, but his battered body slowed him.

The Canadian drew a bead on the bodyguard and fired two shots with the SIG .357. The first shot whizzed by Blankenship's right arm and the second grazed his waist. Blankenship returned fire with his HK-417. When he squeezed the trigger, four bullets blasted from the muzzle almost simultaneously. The Canadian knew Blankenship's weapon was capable of firing over 700 rounds per minute, so he fired back immediately, even though 2 lead bullets had just ripped through his skin. The first bullet went into his thigh, almost exactly where he had shot Jack. The second bullet went through the muscles of his left forearm, causing him to drop the case of money.

The Canadian's second round of shots missed Blankenship completely as the pain in his arm dulled his focus. Blankenship opened fire again, this time with a burst of seven shots, which landed mostly at the Canadian's feet. One passed through his left bicep, rendering his left arm completely useless. They both fired at each other simultaneously. Blankenship emptied his magazine, but the Canadian saved one round as any experienced soldier would.

Blankenship's last two bullets had torn through the Canadian's jacket and punctured his ribs. Blankenship took two slugs to the chest as well. The Canadian knew the bullets landed solidly on Blankenship's torso and watched the bodyguard drop to the ice.

The Canadian's legs wobbled, but he fought the pain and stumbled back to the silver case. He tucked the .357 into its holster and lifted the money with his good arm. Tired legs carried him toward shore where the Marten brothers and Andy had exited the ice, and he collapsed on the river bank. He dropped the heavy case on the ground and fell on his ass into the snow. He stared at Blankenship's body, then cursed as he watched him get to his knees.

"Bulletproof vest," the Canadian said. "I should've friggin known."

Blankenship rose like an old man with arthritis. His breathing was labored as he struggled to inhale and regain his wits. The two slugs hit him like a sledgehammer, breaking a few more ribs on impact. He knew the Canadian had been seriously maimed and would probably bleed to death while he sat on the bank. This satisfied him. Blankenship knew there was one more bullet in the Canadian's pistol and rather than test fate, he began walking back to the woods from where he came—back to the unconscious Stacie. He'd take cover beyond the pines and wait like a vulture, until the Canadian died from his wounds. Then, he could safely move in and acquire the coveted silver case.

Chapter 18 / *A Swallow of Courage*

The cabin smelled like wood smoke and fresh-cut cedar. Andy fetched a few logs of maple from the porch and fed them to the Ben Franklin woodstove in the corner of the small living room. The living room was to the right of the doorway and the kitchen area to the left. A loft with a rustic railing overlooked both rooms, and Paul assumed that was were Andy slept.

The décor was mostly made up of old tools and some pictures framed from barnwood. There was no TV, phone, or even electric lights. Andy walked into the living room, opened the valve on a couple gas lights, and lit the mantles. The glow from the lights illuminated the wood paneled walls and the bearskin rug that hung from one. Once the blinds were drawn up on two windows, the living room was well lit.

"Make yourselves at home, fellas," Andy said.

Paul pulled a wooden rocking chair close to the fire for Eric, but he preferred to stand so he could be closer to the heat radiating from the stovepipe. Jack sat down in Andy's recliner, pulled the lever to open the footrest and propped his injured leg up. Andy fetched a blanket for Eric and a first aid kit for Jack. Andy took a needle and thread out of the first aid kit and struggled to get the thin line through the eye.

"The Jim Beam's on the counter," Andy pointed toward the kitchen with the needle.

Paul retrieved the bourbon whiskey and handed it to Jack. "Here, you look like you could use a swig."

"Thanks." Jack took a drink and set the bottle on an end table next to the recliner. "You know what you're doing?" he asked Andy.

"Hehe, of course I do. I have to stitch myself up once in a while. I would never be able to get an ambulance out here. Have to take care of yourself when you live in the woods."

Paul perused the cabin visually when his eyes fell on Andy's gun cabinet. "Hey, Andy, mind if I look at your guns?"

"Sure, sure, go ahead. Not much of a collection, though."

"Is that a 30-30?" Paul was pointing at the only hunting rifle in the cabinet. It was a lever action Marlin with open sights and mahogany finish. The blue had been almost completely worn off, showing its age.

"Sure is, but I don't have any bullets for it. I ran out last Fall trying to sight it in."

"Got any shells for the twelve gauge shotgun?" Paul asked.

"Oh, I got lots of shells for that. I reload my own. They're in the bottom of the cabinet."

Paul opened the unlocked cabinet and pulled the Mossberg pump shotgun out to admire the beauty of its hardwood stock. The woodgrain was fine, like looking at the side of a ream of paper, but with little waves of imperfection that made it perfect. Some of the wood was dark and some light, but the balance of the two seemed as though it had been planned. Paul imagined a woodworker going through hundreds of pieces of timber until he finally found the one with a grain pattern that suited this weapon.

Jack pushed Andy's hand away from his leg, leaving the needle hanging from the thread that weaved in and out of his skin. He sat straight up. "Paul, don't get any friggin ideas about going back down there. Jesus, these guys are nuts, and you can't go alone."

"Why not? The last thing they're expecting is for one of us to come back. They think we're too afraid to show up and claim that money."

"If we were all in shape to go down, I'd say let's go for it," Jack admitted. "But I can hardly walk. Eric has hypothermia, and Andy…" he paused, trying to think of an excuse for Andy.

"Andy's not going," Paul interrupted.

"I know he's not going…"

"No," Paul interrupted again. "Andy's not going because he's a part of the Canadian's plan."

Jack looked at Andy, and then at Eric, and back to Paul. "What the hell are you talking about?"

"Tell him, Andy," Paul insisted. "Tell them how you're working with this guy who was pretending to be a D.E.C. officer. Tell them how you were part of his plan to bring that plane down."

Andy stood up and stared at the hardwood floor. "I'm not sure what you're implying, Paul. I…I don't' know that guy."

"Bullshit!" Paul stepped toward him and cross-checked him with the shotgun like a professional hockey player. The passive survivalist fell backwards, but his legs caught the coffee table, and

188

he fell onto his back, nearly crushing the furniture under his weight. He sat back up but stayed silent with guilt.

"What makes you think Andy is working with that guy?" Jack asked.

"I've been watching Andy all day," Paul started. "First, I noticed Andy and the Canadian are carrying the same two-way radios. Andy was on that radio several times this morning until the plane crashed. Once the plane crashed, he put the radio away. Then, there's the fact that Andy came to fish but never put a single tip-up in the ice, and he didn't keep any of the perch he caught this morning.

"I also noticed that while he was pretending to be a D.E.C. officer, the Canadian stuck his gun in all our faces several times, but not Andy's. He never pointed the pistol at him once."

"Jesus, Andy, do you know this guy?" Eric asked.

Andy stayed silent.

Paul continued, "And why did he ask for all of our I.D.s, except for Andy's? You were the lookout, weren't you? Once the plane went down, you'd help him find it. Nobody knows these woods and this land better than you, so you were the tracker." The questions turned to statements because Paul could tell by Andy's reaction that he was right.

"Okay, okay," Andy said. "You're right. I'm sorry, nobody was supposed to get hurt. I didn't think there would be anyone else around here today. I wish you guys hadn't gotten involved. I'm so sorry about your leg, Jack. And I never thought the plane would actually crash into the river. We were sure it would go down sooner and land on dry land—in the pines, you know."

"Fuck!" Jack said. He grabbed the thread dangling from his leg and tied it into a knot, stood up, and carried the Jim Beam to the woodstove. He took a long drink and wiped his mouth with his sleeve. "So what do we do now?"

"We need to know who we're dealing with," Paul replied. He walked over to the gun cabinet and started loading shotgun shells into the tubular magazine. He pumped the gun, racking a shell into the chamber. "Andy, who the hell are those guys down there?"

Andy took a moment to collect himself. He gestured for the bottle with an open hand, and Jack obliged him by handing it over.

"The Canadian is my ex-brother-in-law," his voice was solemn and low. He cleared his throat and spoke a little louder. "The other guy? Pff, I have no idea who he is. I think he was a bodyguard from the plane. I don't know how he got off the plane or survived, but he seems to be the real threat."

"Your ex-brother-in-law?"

"Yeah, he used to be married to my sister. They met about 15 years ago; divorced 11 years ago. He contacted me a few weeks ago through a mutual friend, and I called him back. He said he had a plan to save Sophia." Tears came to his eyes as he said the name.

"Sophia?" Jack asked.

"Yeah, my niece; his daughter."

"What do you mean 'save?'"

Andy stood and walked to the only shelf in the living room. He picked up a rustic picture frame with a portrait of a girl not more than 10 years old. She was thin with big green eyes, and two dimples that made her smile look like it was in parenthesis.

He handed the picture to Paul. "This is Sophia. She lives in Mexico with my sister. She's battling cystic fibrosis, and now she may need a lung transplant. The medications, treatments, and therapy put my sister in so much debt she can't even pay her bills anymore. She has no insurance so they might not qualify for the surgery, which is the only thing that will save her life."

"What happens if she doesn't get the surgery?" Eric asked.

"She may survive without it," Andy continued. "But, she'll need a team of doctors and a lifetime of treatment. The drugs are expensive, ya know?"

"Yeah, we know," Paul said. He set the picture back on the shelf. "So, he needs this money to get to Mexico and take care of his daughter."

"Yeah. My sister knows nothing about this, of course. I was going to drive him across the border after he got a fake passport, but if that bodyguard shoots him and takes the money, then there's nothing we can do to save Sophia. We know it's not the best way to save her, but it may be the only way."

Paul's thoughts turned to his niece, Jack's daughter Tara. She lived with her mother in Pennsylvania and was about the same age as Sophia. "Jack, what if this was Tara? Wouldn't you do anything to make her healthy and give her the life she deserves?"

"Of course," Jack said. "But this isn't my daughter or your niece. Are you willing to get yourself killed for a kid you don't even know?"

"Absolutely."

"Yeah, me too," Jack admitted, knowing he wasn't going to stop Paul now. "So, what are we going to do?"

"Why don't I backtrack to the bay? I'll approach from the south. Think you can walk to the north side of the bay?" Paul was looking at Jack's leg.

"I'll be a little slow, but sure, I can get there."

"Once Eric warms up, you guys take Garrison Road around the bay, back to my truck. Wait for me there. Take Andy's walkie-talkie and I'll get the other one from Andy's brother-in-law."

"Ex-brother-in-law," Andy reminded.

"I'll meet you guys at the truck. If the bodyguard comes out before me, take off. Come back and get me in about an hour."

Paul took a seat on the bench at the kitchen table and removed his insulated overalls, freeing himself from the cumbersome bulk. Jack handed him the bottle of Jim Beam, and Paul took a swallow of courage. He patted Andy on the back and then headed for the door with the 12-gauge shotgun in hand. "See you on the other side."

"Thank you, Paul," Andy offered. "I don't expect you to get yourself killed, so be careful."

"The bodyguard could be long gone with the money by now. It's a long shot, but I've gotta take it." With that, Paul opened the door and stepped outside. He knew this was going to be dangerous, but at least he was only putting himself in danger. As he strode through the snow, he was glad Eric and Jack weren't in any shape to come along. They'd be safer if they walked back to the truck and waited for him there.

Paul backtracked down Garrison Road and then cut into the woods where they had exited, following his tracks back toward Bear Bay.

The snow was 13 inches deep, with a few drifts that went above his knees. It was eerily quiet as the snow muffled any sounds the world was making now. The woodpecker had disappeared, taking his annoying sound with him. Paul kept the shotgun pressed tight to his left shoulder; ready to shoot, ready to fight. He paused as the bay came into sight. A loud thumping sound filled his ears, and he thought the woodpecker had returned, until he realized he was hearing his own heartbeat.

Chapter 19 / *Another Way*

The Canadian sat on the ground with his legs straight out in front of him, leaning against a pine tree that curved out over the river 70 degrees. If the tree leaned any further, it would have looked like he was relaxing in a hammock. The tree was large enough to conceal the Canadian from Blankenship's view and gave him a chance to rest and tend to his wounds. His back was to Blankenship, but the Canadian was doubtful the bodyguard would return. Blankenship was pretty beaten and battered, too, so hopefully, he'd had enough and decided to retreat.

Gravity was pulling the Canadian's eyelids downward. He was exhausted and fighting the tendency to blackout. The only thing that kept him awake was the pain in his left arm from the bullet wounds. Surprisingly, the hole in his chest was less painful but more likely to send him to his grave.

He finally lost the battle with his eyelids, but his ears stayed open, listening for anyone trying to approach. As he closed his eyes, he found himself staring at the tombstone that haunted him all the way here.

He was standing so close he could only see the top, so he knelt down and read a single name engraved in the marble—"Sophia."

He traced the letters—a script font debossed a quarter of an inch—with his right index finger. He stepped back to admire the flowers blossoming around the granite monument. He almost smiled at their beauty. The flowers seemed a little brighter, and the grass was the perfect shade of green. The little hummingbird returned, more content than her last visit when she left in a noisy hum of disappointment. Green feathers glimmered in the light. Everything was perfect. Everything was quiet.

He had failed his daughter for the umpteenth time in her short life. He'd never been there for her when she needed him. She counted on her mother for everything and was growing up without knowing who he really was. Someday, if she survived long enough, she would forget about him. All she would remember is the disappointment he brought to her world. The money was going to be his way of making up all the heartache and tears. He thought he was going to fix this, and make up for the time they'd lost together.

The little hummingbird zipped by his head and went behind him.

He pivoted 180 degrees and watched the bird perch herself on a second headstone. A couple of steps put him close enough to see nothing but a skull engraved on the front. He knelt to look closer.

The skull was rough and incomplete, as if the artist had rushed the engraving to meet a strict deadline. The granite was glossy with a mirror-like finish, but the only reflection he could see was his own, overlaying the edgy skull staring back at him.

A branch cracked in front of him, and a surge of adrenaline forced him from his dream.

"Blankenship?" the Canadian mechanic asked in a weak voice. There was no answer.

A noisy grouse took flight and zig-zagged through the trees toward him. It sailed 10 feet above his head toward the open ice, and then abrubtly turned right and flew back into the security of the thick evergreens. Something, or someone, had spooked the grouse, which put him on high alert. He assumed Blankenship was coming to finish him off. He pulled his pistol from his holster, ready to die, but determined to live.

****

Paul's stomach knotted like a pretzel when he thought about what he might have to do. He never thought he'd be in a situation that might cause him to use a gun on another person. He wanted to avoid that at all costs, even if it meant losing the money. "Losing the money," he thought about the notion. It wasn't even his money to lose. He found the money in the plane, but it belonged to someone else. Someone corrupt, sure, but never-the-less, someone else, not him. Did the Canadian have more right to that money than Paul? No. No, he did not. Did the plane's owner have more right to the money? No, he didn't deserve it.

Paul knew the right thing—the morally correct thing—to do, was to turn the money over to the police and forget it ever existed. But shit, most of the police were corrupt, too. How could he be sure they could be trusted? He wished Stacie's Uncle Ernie was there—he'd know what to do.

He crested the last hill near the bay and ducked behind a fallen log to study the scene below. There was some blood on the ice, but devoid of maniacal Canadians trying to kill each other. He knew the serenity was false and decided to sidestep along the hill to further observe. On his third step, a grouse popped up from behind some beech whips, scaring Paul so much that he nearly pulled the trigger of the shotgun. His heart pounded harder than the bird's wings beat the winter air.

Paul couln't help but to follow the bird with his eyes. It shot toward the river, zig-zagging through the trees and into the bay. Then it turned 90 degrees to the right and came back to the woods. Paul knew the bird's noisy getaway announced his presence, so he stood erect and scanned the woods between himself and the ice.

Thirty yards in front of him, Paul could see the Canadian supine against the leaning tree. The Canadian's eyes were scanning the forest until they locked on Paul. To Paul's surprise, the Canadian holstered his pistol and relaxed when he realized it was not Blankenship who had spooked the grouse. The Canadian watched Paul descend the hill with a shouldered shotgun. The shotgun's front sight stayed pinned on the Canadian's chest as Paul meandered down.

The Candian had shed one of his shirts and tore pieces off to bandage his wounds. A bloody knife, used to remove one of the slugs, rested on his lap. His teeth were crimson from coughing up the fluid that filled one of his lungs. The red liquid seeped into his red beard, hiding the gray and giving the injured man a savage appearance.

He made eye contact with Paul a couple of times as if to say, "I see you coming. I'm not surprised." But mostly, he just ignored Paul's approach. Each man knew the other was not a threat.

"You okay?" Paul asked more out of reflex than actual concern.

197

"Yeah. I'm…I'm okay. That friggin Blankenship got off a couple of lucky shots. Frigger should go back to Ottawa and play the lottery with his luck."

"Where is he now? Did he leave with the money?"

"Nope," the Canadian pulled the case from beside the tree and set it on his lap. "I guess this is what you came back for, eh? Finish me off and take the money for yourself?"

"No."

The Canadian squinted in confusion.

Paul walked closer and took a seat on a dead log. He scanned the bay, looking for Blankenship, as well as the words to explain why he came back. "Andy told me why you were doing this. He confessed to everything."

"Andy told you he was helping me?"

"Yeah. I had to drag it out of him, but I put the pieces together myself. I knew the two of you were conspiring together."

"I used to be married to his sister. Man, she was pretty. Looks nothing like Andy," he laughed and choked at the same time. "She had passion. It was contagious, ya know? Some women are like that. She'd get fired up about things and, well, I guess I just pissed her off too many times."

"You have a little girl with her?"

The Canadian's eyes glazed over, and then he looked away to hide his weakness. He cleared his throat of blood and phlegm. "I haven't been much of a father. Haven't been in her life since she was a baby."

He pulled a picture of Sophia out of his pocket. It was the same one Andy had in a frame, but smaller. Paul guessed it was a school portrait based on the cheesy pose and cheap background. The Canadian continued, "She's still my baby, eh. I thought I'd have more time to make things right, get to see her grow up and give me grandkids someday. I'm not sure how long she'll live, but I want the rest of the time she has to be special—fun, with memories of us doing things together."

"I know," Paul admitted.

"Do you? Do you have kids, Paul?" It was the first time the Canadian called him by name. Paul kept watching over the frozen river bay.

"No. No, I wish I did. My wife and aren't in any situation to have kids right now—financially."

"Ha!" the Canadian blurted. "You'll never be financially ready for kids. No one is. They're expensive little boogers. But dammit, they're worth it."

The Canadian gave him a sober look. "Take some of this money," he nodded at the case. "Change your situation and start the family you want. Once you hold that precious little bundle in your arms, you'll completely understand why I'm doing this. You'll love that child more than anything, and you'd give your left arm to protect them." He looked at his left arm. The blood had slowed, but the pain advanced as his adrenaline wore off.

"No, you're going to keep that money. You're going to reunite with your daughter and make some memories with her. Hopefully, you can save her. I'll find another way."

"I'm never going to see my daughter again." He stared at the picture as if it could talk back to him. "I keep seeing a tombstone in my mind. For days now... I see it, and I know it's hers. I've been using that vision to fuel my fire—to push myself. I've dug as deep as I could to find the strength to do this. Hell, I even had to kill a man last night after he tried to rob me." He spat blood into the fresh snow. "He was just a kid himself. Brought me across the border and then he pulled a gun on me—a gun. Why did he do that?"

"Maybe he didn't realize how far you'd go to protect what was yours."

"That was too far. I have to live with his death now, and that's a shitty thing. The worse part is that that kid probably died for nothing. I probably won't get this money to Sophia or ever see her again. I've failed."

"No, you haven't failed. You've got the money, and we can get it to her. You just need to stay alive so we can get you medical attention."

"I'm not going to make it out of these woods, Paul. Blankenship made sure of that."

"If not, I'll take the money to Andy. He can take it to his sister."

"You're a good guy," the Canadian admitted. "I'm sorry things happened the way they did. You and your brothers shouldn't have been caught up in this shit. I imagined no one would be around when that plane went down."

Paul scanned the wounds on the Canadian's body,."Can you walk?"

"I can try."

"Then let's get the hell out of here. Andy has medical supplies in his cabin. It's only a couple minutes from here. Come on, I'll help you," Paul grabbed the Canadian's hand and helped him to his feet. Paul took the hefty case so the Canadian could use his only good arm to lean on Paul's left shoulder. They started up the hill, toward Andy's cabin, when a voice began to yell across the ice.

It was Blankenship. Peering from behind a large pine on the other side of the bay. He shouted from the shadows, "I'm coming for my money, you sonavabitches!"

The words seemed to echo in the the Canadian's ears, thumping his brain, and skewing his balance. He grabbed a small beech tree for stability. The snow and trees blurred around him as he focused on finding the source of the noise. His adrenaline arose again as he watched Blankenship enter the opening and expose himself from the security of the standing timber.

"Do you have any more bullets in that thing?" Paul asked, nodding at the pistol holstered on the Canadian's side.

"One."

"One might be all it takes. If we can get Blankenship to follow us in the woods, I can distract him with a couple of shots, and you finish what you started."

The Canadian nodded in agreement, but looked out at the bodyguard advancing. "What about her?"

Blankenship was not alone. Stacie marched in front of the big man as he held the .22 caliber pistol to the back of her head. His fist held her collar, steering her like a dog caught by Animal Control. The .22 pistol pointing to the back of her head forced her to comply. They crossed the ice silent and slow, keeping their eyes ahead. Stacie's heart pounded with fear—not just for herself, but for her husband and baby. Her wet cheeks were cold in the wind, and she sniffled as she walked. She couldn't believe how heavy her boots felt as she heaved one, then the other, over and over to get across the bay. Her stomach spasmed in protest from the exertion, but she was able to keep herself from spilling its contents.

"Come on," the Canadian insisted. "He can't use someone we don't know as leverage. We'll get him to follows us and ambush him in the woods."

Paul watched the woman stride across the ice. The way her shoulders rolled, the sway of her hips, and the swing of her arms gave her identity away. Paul would recognize that walk anywhere.

"Actually, I think that's my wife." He was calm. His voice was low, and he had an overwhelming sense of defeat. He lowered the shotgun while his complexion went as white as the ground he was standing on. He could feel himself squeezing the stock of the gun so hard his hand began to go numb. As they moved closer, Paul could see the fear in Stacie's eyes as she stared straight ahead.

How dare he.

How dare that bastard to bring her into this.

Chapter 20 / *I'm Coming for You*

Paul stood with one foot on the ice, the other on the frozen ground. Blankenship was to his right and the Canadian was to his left. He felt torn in the moment, cursing the predicament he was caught in. The money could save the life of the Canadian's daughter, or at least give her quality of life for what time remained. She needed the money, sure, but he needed his wife. Would Blankenship let them go if he handed over the money?

He had to take the chance. Had to try.

Paul didn't look back. He stepped completely onto the ice and spoke to the man that was now to his back. "I'm sorry."

Blankenship and Stacie were now 60 yards away.

The Canadian pulled the pistol from its holster and switched the safety button to the firing position. "Paul, drop the case."

"You won't shoot me," Paul said. He took one more step onto the ice without even turning around to see the threat behind him.

"Paul! Paul, don't give him that money! I will shoot you!"

"Bullshit," Paul said. "You're not willing to spill anymore blood. You did what you had to do, now I'm doing what I have to do." Even though he said the words, Paul couldn't get his legs to work.

The wind blew from the west, carrying a whisper across the pines, and into his left ear. He couldn't make out the words or decipher the language, but he was sure the whisper was telling him to save his wife. Paul felt as though another presence was with them on the frozen bay. He looked through the boughs to his right only to see the uninhabited forest. He wished he had Eric's keen eyes now. Someone else was there; but where?

"He's going to kill you both, Paul," the Canadian said. "Once he has the money, he'll kill any witnesses."

"What can I do? If I give it to you, then he'll shoot my wife. I can't live with that. I'd rather die than be without her!"

Paul's world went silent. His breathing became shallow. Cold sweat trickled down his forehead. What would Stacie want? Would she be ashamed of Paul for choosing her over a young girl with cystic fibrosis? Would she want Paul to run and take the money? Or would he be the husband he vowed to be and stick with his wife "for better or worse?"

Blankenship decided for him when he yelled again, "Bring me the fucking money, or I shoot her and the baby she's carrying!" He was pointing the pistol at her abdomen now.

Stacie must have seen the look of confusion on Paul's face. She forced a little smile and peered up at Paul with watery eyes. She nodded to reaffirm that it was true. "I'm sorry, honey. I came up here to tell you, but I pictured it to be a much more beautiful moment than this." She made a little gesture with her hands, like a magician. "Surprise."

Paul squeezed the shotgun stock even harder.

Blankenship was now 45 yards from Paul.

Three men. Three guns. One outcome.

Paul felt a hand on his shoulder. He spun around with the barrel of the shotgun shoved under the Canadian's chin and ready to blow the Canadian's ass back to Ottawa.

"Give him the money and save your wife and baby. I can't let one innocent kid die to save another."

"I'll give him the money, but that doesn't mean he has to get away with it. Once Stacie and I are clear, put a bullet in that asshole," Paul said.

"You read my mind," the Canadian smirked. "I'll tuck back into the trees so he can't see me. Once you're out of the way, he's history. I'll get the money back from him somehow. One way or another, Blankenship's not getting off this river alive." He sat back down in the snow. The loss of blood was starting to take its toll on him. His eyes grew heavy, and blackness invaded his sight.

Paul stepped away from the bleeding man on the river bank and started out toward his wife and her captor. The wind whispered once more, and Paul felt a storm building inside him. He could see the smug look on Blankenship's face, and he wanted nothing more than to remove it with the 12-gauge turkey-load chambered in the shotgun.

"Leave the shotgun," Blankenship directed.

Paul took to one knee and gently set the gun on the ice. He moved slow, not wanting to startle Blankenship and cause him to pull the trigger. Blankenship held Stacie in place and waited for

Paul to come a little further. The ice cracked under Paul's weight, and he realized he was just eight feet from the hole where the plane rested.

He walked straight toward Stacie, placing his steps carefully on the frail surface. Their eyes were locked on each other. Neither could look away. It reminded Paul of their wedding day when Stacie made her way down the church aisle, and he couldn't take his eyes off of her. Only now, he was the one walking toward her, and their eyes were not locked in love, but in fear. It took all his strength to keep from running to her, but he kept his restraint.

When he was 12 feet away, Paul set the case on the ice. His unblinking eyes were still locked on Stacie's.

Blankenship kept inching forward. "Move back."

Paul followed his instructions and backed away from the money. Blankenship advanced and ordered Stacie to pick up the case. She squatted and lifted the prize and Blankenship began tugging on her collar in the reverse direction. His arm was straight, and he hunched to try and hide behind the pretty blonde.

"You've got the money," Paul yelled. "Now let her go!"

Blankenship's smile was maniacal. He kept moving backward with the .22 still trained on Paul's torso. "She's coming with me—for insurance purposes. If you try to follow me, I'll put a bullet in her pretty skull."

The bodyguard and his hostage were 30 feet from Paul when a shot rang out. Blankenship cried out and grabbed the right side of his neck instinctively with the same hand holding the gun.

The Canadian had fired his last bullet and put a groove in the side of Blankenship's neck that just missed the carotid artery. Stacie saw the opportunity to throw a reverse elbow into Blankenship's abdomen. She tried to bolt, but the powerful left arm never released its grip.

Blankenship took aim at the conifer forest, but couln't find the elusive target that had just put a chunk of lead through his collar. He screamed at Paul and decided to fire at the only target in sight. He pulled Stacie tight against his body, took aim and fired. The first bullet whizzed by Paul's left ear. The second came right behind it, but Blankenship over-corrected his elevation and caught Paul in the left leg. The bullet grazed flesh, avoiding muscle or bone.

"Run!" Stacie screamed at her husband.

There was nowhere for Paul to run. He was caught out in the open, standing on a frozen river with nothing to hide behind. His instincts kicked in and he dove to his right as more bullets sailed past. Paul rolled with his momentum and back onto his feet again. He stayed moving and headed for the one thing that had always given him a sense of security—water. He sprung off the edge of the ice, dove toward the wrecked plane, and prepared for the shocking cold that was sure to come.

As Paul hit the water, one bullet found its target and nailed his right hand, fracturing a metacarpal bone. The icy water hurt almost as much as the gunshot wound as he skewered the surface and went deep enough to avoid another bullet. He pointed his fingers straight down to ensure the dive was deep and to avoid hitting the wrecked plane. The rounds hitting the surface were the only sounds Paul could hear. He knew the small caliber bullets would skip off the surface of the water—something he learned in his teen years when he would shoot frogs at the pond behind his parent's house.

He was safe, for the moment.

Paul wasn't sure what would happen when he resurfaced, but he needed to go back up and fight. Hopefully, Blankenship had used all of his ammunition. Paul studied the plane and thought about where he would surface. He pulled himself down the length of the plane, plunging to the bottom. From here, Paul could see Blankenship and Stacie—two blurred shadows through the translucent ice making there way toward the hole. Blankenship still had his arm around Stacie, holding her so she could not run. Stacie was still alive, and that was all that mattered.

Stacie knew Paul could stay submerged for several minutes. She used to marvel at his swimming abilities which sometimes scared the hell out of her when he wouln't resurface for some time. She bit down into Blankenship's right arm and threw more elbows. She thought about Uncle Ernie and what the monster grasping her had done to him. She wished she had his strength right now and could beat the life out of Blankenship.

But she did not.

Blankenship flung her to the side. Stacie spun, slipped, and fell on her back. Blankenship pointed the pistol at her chest and pulled the trigger.

Click. Click.

The gun was empty, and it infuriated him. He threw the pistol aside and checked to see if Paul was coming back. The water was black and void of any life. It appeared the ice fisherman was gone for good; drowned in the river or taken by the current.

Paul heard the pistol hit the ice. What happened? Was the gun empty? He could see Stacie's silhouette through the ice. She was crab-walking away from Blankenship who stared down into the dark abyss of the river. Satisfied that Paul was not coming back to the surface, Blankenship turned his attention back to the woman on the ice.

Paul needed a weapon. A rock from the bottom, glass from the plane's broken window—anything that would give him an advantage against the skilled bodyguard trying to kill his wife. He swam into the plane, searching for a loose tool or steel part to aid his assault. The plane was empty. He swam to the cockpit and searched the co-pilot seat. There was nothing there of use.

The body of the skinny pilot occupied the other half of the cockpit. Paul wanted to avoid the morbid image and did his best not to look. Ozzy's head was crooked against the ceiling while his legs seemed to be stuck under the plan's yoke. The weightless body drifted back and forth in the current as the water swirled through the broken windshield. The pilot's seat was the last place to look. Paul reluctantly grabbed the body and gave it a little pull to clear his view in his desperate search for a weapon.

There it was. Not a broken piece of the plane, or some tool that fell free during the crash, but a gun—a friggin gun.

Paul's hands shook from the excitement of his find. He no longer cared what Ozzy's battered body looked like or feared to disrespect the deceased pilot. He spun the body around, unbuckled the holster, and took the Taurus .38 Special revolver from Ozzy's side.

"Please, have bullets," Paul thought. He opened the cylinder to see five rounds nestled inside. He'd have four shots to kill Blankenship and one for the Canadian if necessary—although Paul didn't think that was likely.

He almost smiled at the luck of finding the pistol. He jerked, put his feet on the dashboard, and pushed away. He glided through the plane and out the cargo doors.

"I'm coming for you, baby," Paul thought with the image of Stacie in his mind. "I'm coming for you, too, asshole," as he thought about Blankenship.

Paul's optimism was cut short after he exited the plane. He could see the two silhouettes above had merged into one. Blankenship was attacking Stacie. Paul began to rise when the current from the nearby brook plowed into him like a truck. He wasn't holding onto the plane, and the pistol in his hand hindered his swimming. He was being pushed downriver—the opening above him began to look further away. A younger Paul could have fought through the current, beat the river in a shoving match, but his heavy winter clothes hindered his grace. He felt clumsy and uncoordinated, unlike the streamline swimmer he used to be.

"No!" he screamed, though no one could hear him underwater.

Paul could see Stacie's legs flailing on the ice as Blankenship's attack endured. Paul fought the river, fought his emotions, and fought for his family. As powerful of a swimmer as he was, he was no match for the the current. He pulled his hands frantically through the water, but the river pushed back. The river current was steady and unyielding like a train with no end. Paul could not get back to the surface. He would drown—an ironic death for a championship swimmer—and the last thing he would ever see was the murder of his wife.

Chapter 22 / *Hurts Like Hell*

Andy Kessler turned the key, but the stubborn old truck refused to start. The starter seemed to engage but wasn't cranking with enough speed to turn the engine and fire the cylinders. The truck's battery was too weak. He exited the vehicle, popped open the hood, and then went to his tool shed to retrieve a trickle charger. Then he went to the porch on the back of the cabin and started a generator. A long extension cord was plugged into the generator and the charger. It would take a few hours to revive the battery with the charger, so Andy went in to give the Marten's the bad news.

"Battery's dead on my truck, fellas," Andy said as he entered the cabin. "Give it a couple hours to charge, and then I can drive you down to Paul's truck."

Jack and Eric both knew they didn't have a couple of hours to wait for a ride. Paul could be in danger, and they needed to leave. They could walk to Paul's truck in 25 minutes if Jack's leg didn't slow them down too much.

"We need to get to Paul's truck," Eric remarked. He was buttoning the heavy flannnel shirt he was wearing—a donation from Andy's closet. The shirt was too large in the chest and shoulders and fell four inches short at the wrists, but it would keep him warm on the walk back to the truck. He finished with the bottons and helped Jack out of the recliner.

Andy watched the two brothers slip back into their boots. They seemed to do everything in unison, like it was a rehearsed act. Their moves always seemed to be syncronized, and Andy realized that it was because the siblings knew each other so well, and thought so much alike. Andy had no brothers and had very little contact with his sister. He envied the relationship the Martens had and wished he had brothers of his own. If he had brothers, he might not live such a reclusive life. Would anyone risk their life to help him? No, he assumed.

"You fellas sure you're ready to go back out there?" Andy asked them both.

"We have to," Eric responded. "That's our brother out there."

"We've got to go check on him," Jack implored. "We all might be dead by the end of the day, but we'll be dead together," "We'll make our way to Haystack Rock. If Paul's not there soon, we'll go back to the bay to find him."

"If you make it to the ice, there's a .22 magnum rifle in my sled," Andy offered. "The magazine is full—should be six rounds in it, plus one in the chamber. I keep it in there for shootin' grouse or coyotes."

"Thanks," Eric opened the door, and the two Martens headed out into the winter. The snow had stopped falling, and the air temperature had pushed up three degrees.

Jack and Eric made their way north on Garrison Road and passed where they had exited the woods. "Let's stay on the road," Jack advised, "It'll be easier walking."

"How's the leg feel?" Eric asked.

"Hurts like hell. I don't think Andy and Jim Beam are very good doctors."

Both men wished they had transportation, but they were only three-quarters of a mile from where Paul had parked the truck. The road curved around the bay with a 300 yard buffer of forest in between. They could almost see the bay from their location since the trees were void of their foliage, but a thick row of evergreens grew along the river, hindering their view.

"Are you still cold?" Jack asked Eric.

"Not too bad.As long as we keep moving, I'll stay warm enough."

The two brothers persevered down the unplowed road. The sound of their boots scuffing along was the only noise they could hear. They weren't sure if the silence was reassuring, or cause for concern. Jack leaned against a cherry tree and cinched his bandage tighter. His sharp ears listened before the two brothers resumed their hike. Another quarter of a mile and they would be at Haystack Rock, and hopefully, Paul would exit the ice from that side.

Snow began to fall again, but the warm temperature caused it to mix with light rain. Jack and Eric continued their march in the unwelcome sleet.

Haystack Rock came into view as they crested a knoll. The snow around the rock showed footprints that were too fresh to belong to the Marten brothers. Although his adrenaline was high, Jack needed to stop and rest his leg. He lit a cigarette. "Why don't you go ahead and bring Paul's truck up here. I'll wait to see if he comes out."

215

Eric watched Jack for a moment. Jack was studying the footprints that circled Haystack Rock. Something caught Eric's attention, and he walked over to a stump and picked up a small cooler that lay beside it. He unzipped the top, surprised to find six cold beers inside.

"Someone else has been here." Eric held up the cooler for Jack to see.

"And their tracks lead into Bear Bay, but they never came out," Jack mused.

Eric turned his head over his left shoulder. "Probably hunting rabbits. Or, maybe someone came to investigate the plane crash."

"Maybe. Those aren't D.E.C. or State Police boots. The tread looks more like snow boots. And one set is either a kid's or a woman's."

Eric looked closer at the two distinctly different tracks. "I think you're right. Let's follow them in and see if we can find out who it is. Maybe they can help."

They followed the tracks off Garrison Road, which lead them back toward the river. Eric followed as Jack studied the prints. The sleet continued to fall with a sound similar to someone playing with cling wrap. Jack kept his head down as he studied where the man and woman trekked. Eric's eyes scanned ahead in case they encountered Blankenship on his way out of the woods.

They hadn't gone more than 30 yards when they were halted by a faint voice.

"Over here," the voice whispered.

Jack held up a fist to stop. Eric had been trained at a young age to recognize the hand symbol from years of tracking deer with his brothers and their father.

"Did you hear that?" Jack asked. He held his breath as he listened for the sound again.

"Over there! Someone's on the ground!" Eric pointed through the trees.

Their hearts raced with the horrible thought that it might be Paul, but they realized the color of the clothes was different from what Paul was wearing. They hopped over a couple logs and pushed through some snow-covered hemlocks to reach the stranger, only to realize that it was no stranger at all.

Ernie Bates had crawled out of the thick evergreens where he'd been investigating pieces of the plane and was attacked by Mason Blankenship. He collapsed 20 yards from the trail that led to the bay. Blood covered the side of his head. He grabbed for a small beech tree to pull himself off his knees but collapsed again. His hip was impeding his progress to make it out of the woods, and he was fighting with the loss of blood and hypothermia.

Jack and Eric rushed to his side and propped Stacie's uncle against a fallen log.

"Jesus, Ernie, how the hell did you get here?" Jack asked.

Ernie struggled for breath and was clearly in shock. He pointed a shaky finger toward the bay. "St…Stacie. She was taken by some guy from the plane crash."

"Oh shit!" Eric muttered. "Stacie's here with you?"

"Yeah," Ernie replied. "Her and I were going to see Paul. She wanted to tell him about the baby."

"What baby?" Jack and Eric asked simultaneously.

"Her baby. Their baby. She's pregnant and wants to tell him."

"What happened to you?" Jack asked. "What happened to your head?"

"Shot," Ernie muttered. "Some big guy came out of the woods. We tussled a bit, and I was going to kick his ass." He paused to try and remember how he went from dominating the brawl to laying flat on his back. "Sonavabitch pulled a pistol and shot me."

"Good thing you're a tough old bastard, huh?" Jack tried to lighten the mood.

Then the three of them froze in fear. They all listened as several shots echoed from the bay. The sound was faint, a small caliber firearm for sure. It was nothing like the HK from Blankenship or the .357 the Canadian was shooting. Their years of hunting and shooting told them the sound came from a .22 caliber pistol or rifle. But who's?

A couple more shots echoed in the distance.

"What the hell is going on?" Eric had no idea that the sound he was hearing was Blankenship firing his pistol at Paul.

"I don't know, but it's not the shotgun Paul was carrying."

218

"Think he's okay?" Eric asked.

"The big fella," Ernie started, "had a small pistol. Maybe a .22. I think that's what we just heard."

"Eric, we've gotta find Stacie!" Jack exclaimed.

Eric was on the move before Jack could finish the sentence. "Stay with Ernie, I'll find Stacie." He took off in a sprint, darting between the pines and crisscrossing over Stacie and Blankenship's tracks. His clothes were still damp and made his stride sluggish, but he persevered. He ran with fear in his veins. He ran like he'd never ran before. And he ran with purpose.

Eric realized that when they saw Blankenship on the ice, he was alone. Stacie was never with him at the bay. Where was Stacie then? Were they too late? Was she already dead?

Eric knew it might be too late. He raced even harder, thinking about how his brother would react to the news.

Chapter 23 / *Never Give Up*

Paul was starting to feel the temperature of the water affect his muscles. Blood leaked from the hole in his hand. His fingers were stiff, and his back was teasing to cramp up. He tucked the .38 Special into his belt, flipped around and made a bold decision. A few powerful dolphin kicks, working with the current, sent him down the river. His big hands pulled through the water as he kicked with every bit of power he could muster.

He was swimming harder than he had ever swum before— away from his struggling wife and her attacker. It was a risk, but he knew it was the only chance to get back to the surface. He went deep so that he could see the fishing holes. The light barely penetrated the water at 12 feet down, but this helped him see the holes that he and his brothers had drilled through the ice.

The perforations in the ice formed a straight line, spaced 20 feet or more apart. The dull sunlight shined through the holes, lighting them up like street lights above. Paul followed the path until he found his target.

The large hole in the ice from the plane's initial impact was just 30 more feet, so Paul pointed his fingers upward, and dolphin kicked twice to rise to the surface. His lungs were burning now, begging for fresh oxygen, but he denied them the pleasure. He began to exhale, relieving the tired lungs from the build-up of carbon dioxide as he approached the ice above him.

Paul's head finally broke the surface of the water, and he grabbed the broken and jagged ice to keep himself from slipping under. Once he oriented himself, he found Stacie and Blankenship in his vision.

Paul knew it would take him about ten seconds to run across the ice, but he was optimistic that Stacie could hold on that long. He put both hands on the ice and pulled himself up, but not enough. He tried again and again. His tired muscles seemed to reject his mental commands. Blood spilled from his hand and coated the slick ice, making the surface even more slippery. He could not get out of the water.

Frustration grew in his head. He was a champion swimmer. He'd picked himself out of the pool a thousand times with the ease of a seal. He realized that was 9 years and 15 pounds ago. To add to the incumbrance, his wet clothes added another 20 pounds and the slippery ice gave him no assistance.

Paul propped himself the best he could on his elbows. The broken ice stabbed his armpits, and he knew this was as far as he was going to get out of the water. He pulled the Taurus revolver from his waistband and cocked the hammer.

Blankenship was straddling Stacie with his back to Paul. Luckily, Blankenship's long arms prevented him from having to bend forward too far which left his back exposed as Paul's target.

Paul peered down the four-inch barrel, lined up the front sight on Blankenship's back and squeezed the trigger.

Boom!

The shot sailed high and left, missing Blankenship's head by a foot. He readjusted and compensated for his error and squeezed another shot from the pistol.

221

Boom!

The elevation was perfect—he hoped—but the bullet still went left. He figured the broken bone in his hand was causing him to pull left with each shot. Three rounds were left in the cylinder, and he needed to make them count. He peeked down the barrel again, readjusted his grip, and centered Blankenship in the front sight. The tight grip on the pistol was agonizing to his right hand, but he kept the pressure and blocked the pain from his mind. The distance from the barrel to its target was 70 yards—a difficult shot even with a rifle. Right now, Paul needed a miracle to hit Blankenship and stop him from taking the life of his wife and the baby growing in her womb.

Boom!

Again, the bullet missed.

Paul's numb body was cramping. His entire body violently shook from the cold, but his hands were steady. He envisioned his father standing behind him, giving directions to shoot. "Take a deep breath. Now exhale half of it slowly. Hold it. Squeeze the trigger gently; let it surprise you."

He followed his father's guidance.

Boom! Thwap!

Paul heard the bullet hit Blankenship in the middle of his back. The bodyguard reeled with an arching back. He let go of Stacie's throat long enough for her to gasp for air. The bodyguard had the wind knocked out of him, and now he was the one struggling to breathe. But when Blankenship saw how far Paul was shooting from, he decided the fisherman had just gotten lucky.

Enraged, he continued his attack on Stacie, and when he finished, the husband would be next.

Paul realized Blankenship was wearing a bulletproof vest. The little victory of hitting his target slipped away, as he would soon slip under the ice. He had one shot left. One chance to save his wife. One bullet to put through that sonovabitch's head.

Boom!

Blankenship felt the fifth and final shot rip through the back of his left arm. The tricep muscles exploded and the humerus bone split in half. The arm was useless now, and he gave up choking Stacie for a moment. Stacie seized the opportunity to suck in more oxygen before his right hand clamped around her throat again.

"I'm gonna squeeze the fuckin life out of you, bitch. Then I'm going to finish your husband!"

He was so close to her face, drool spilled from his mouth as he salivated from the thought of victory. He was sweating now, and she could smell his rotten breath in her nostrils.

Stacie's eyes closed. She didn't want his face to be the last thing she ever saw. She thought visions of Paul and her baby would flood her mind. She thought her whole life was going to flash before her eyes—wasn't that what was supposed to happen? She relaxed her body and waited for the visions. The quick slideshow of her life never played.

Instead, a green coffee cup flashed into her mind. She saw herself sitting at Aunt Marie's table with her hands gripped around the warm mug. She read the words she had traced with her finger earlier that day. "Never give up on the things you love."

Her eyes popped open; adrenaline flooded her veins. She was not going to give up on her baby. She was not going to give up on Paul.

Stacie straight-armed Blankenship's bony chin with her right palm. His bottom and top teeth smashed together. The attacker straightened with the blow, giving Stacie enough room to bring her right leg up and hook his left shoulder. Blankenship could not stop her leg after Paul's bullet shattered his upper arm bone. Stacie grabbed his limp arm and twisted. The bone fragments sounded like raw spaghetti cracking inside his arm. With all her strength, she pushed him back with her leg.

The bodyguard flipped backward, releasing his grip and cracked his head against the solid ice. They both rolled away from each other. Stacie gasped for air while Blankenship shook off a minor concussion. Paul watched the drama unfold, helpless in the hole that he was sure would be his grave.

"Thatta girl," Paul whispered with his weakening voice. "Kick his ass."

But Blankenship wasn't done yet. He struggled to his knees and smiled at Paul. Paul tried to fight his way out of the ice again. He could feel the current, although slower here, pulling at his legs and threatening to drag him under the ice. He tried to kick his feet, to give him a push, but the heavy boots hindered the effort. The loss of blood and hypothermia were starting to take their toll. Muscles cramped throughout his body and his legs were resisting his commands to keep kicking.

Why was Blankenship so smug? When the answer came, Paul had regretted the question.

Blankenship held up the shotgun that Paul had brought with him from Andy's. The gun was hidden in the snow until Blankenship rolled over and inadvertently landed on it. He held it so Paul could see the prize in his hands.

"The Canadian was right," Paul thought. "He is a lucky bastard." Paul had one shot left with the pistol. He'd wait for Blankenship to stand and present himself as a larger target.

Blankenship took his time. He taunted Paul by pointing the gun in his direction. Then he pointed it at Stacie and back at Paul—a sadistic game of eeny, meany, miny, mo.

"Come and get me, you bastard!" Paul screamed, forcing his voice to work. "Come on! What are waiting for?" He wanted Blankenship to forget about Stacie. He wanted the battered bodyguard to make his way across the ice. Then he'd deliver the final bullet into Blankenship's skull.

Blankenship didn't take the bait. He set the gun upright on the ice and used it to prop himself up. Paul's eyes scanned the woods. Where was the Canadian?

The Canadian was nowhere to be found. Paul took aim with Ozzy's pistol, but struggled to keep the front sight trained on its target. He was shaking uncontrollably now.

Blankenship just stared at Paul with an audacious smile across his lips. He paused to regain his breath and find a small surge of energy, but his hesitation was a mistake.

Stacie had already recovered from Blankenship's attack.

Blankenship wasn't the only one to get lucky and find something in the snow. He never saw Stacie sneak up behind him. He never saw her pick up the five-foot-long steel ice spud. And, he never saw it coming when she swung it with all her might, breaking two vertebrae in his neck.

Blankenship hit the ice limp. His torso rolled to the left, and he laid half-twisted, looking to the sky. Stacie dropped the heavy ice spud and collapsed to her knees in exhaustion and relief.

Paul smiled and whispered as if she could hear him, "Thatta girl." Tears burst from his eyes at the satisfying sight of watching his wife kneel in victory.

Paul's head slumped to the ice as the exhaustion overtook him. He'd been in the water too long and used every ounce of energy trying to free himself from the frigid trap that threatened to take him under. His boots, full of water, weighed him down as the current pulled. His grip slipped, and he felt himself going under. His face was just inches away from being completely submerged.

Stacie saw Paul sinking out of sight. Somehow, she recovered from Blankenship's assault like someone had flipped a switch. She sprung from her knees and bolted across the ice with all of her speed. Within 12 seconds, she was at the hole, only to see Paul lose his grip and drop under the water. He kicked weakly at the dark water when he saw her standing over him, but he was succumbing to the unyielding power of the Raquette River.

Stacie dove onto her belly and reached into the 40 degree water. She was able to grab three fingers on Paul's ungloved hand, but the grip was starting to break. Then she heard footsteps—no, foot stomps! Boots running across the ice, thumping louder and louder as someone approached.

Stacie didn't dare take her eyes off Paul. She didn't care if it was Blankenship coming to finish her off. Without Paul, she had nothing to live for. A voice cried out that she could hardly hear, as her focus was on Paul. The grip loosened more, and then it broke completely. Her husband sank out of sight. Stacie felt as though her heart was tied to Paul because she could feel it being pulled from her chest.

The voice cried out again. Stacie finally looked up as Eric reached her side. He was holding the rope he had braided from fishing line earlier and handed an end to Stacie.

"Hold this!" Without hesitation, he jumped back into the cold water for the third time in one day. Eric didn't have to swim far. He could see Paul drifting backward with the current, one arm still outreached toward his wife. Eric swam toward his older brother and wrapped the line around his wrist. He tied it off as fast as possible, knowing Paul didn't have much longer.

Once the line was secure, Eric used the rope to pull himself back toward daylight while Stacie held tight. As soon as Stacie saw Eric returning to the hole, she knew the weight at the end of the line had to be her husband. She began pulling hand over hand, nearly pulling herself into the water. Eric treaded water while holding the edge of the ice and helped Stacie by pulling, too. Stacie cried as conflicting emotions swallowed her. She was happy that Paul was coming back to her as she pulled, but she was also afraid that the rope might break any second and she'd lose him again. She wrapped the rope around her arm, determined to maintain her grip. The rope cinched around her wrist and sawed into her skin, but she blocked the pain and continued reeling in her husband. If her husband reversed direction now, he'd pull her with him, but that was a chance she was willing to take.

At that moment, Paul and the baby were both attached to her by a cord, and she made herself a promise to never let either of them go. She promised she would give her life to either of them, if necessary.

Paul's head came to the surface, and Eric hoisted him as high as he could. Paul coughed and then sucked in a breath of fresh air.

"He's okay," Eric was thankful. "He's going to be okay."

"Paul!" Stacie cried. "Paul, are you all right?"

"Yeah, I'm okay," his voice was weak. "Thanks, Eric. Thanks."

Paul was almost delirious in his exhausted state. A smile came across his lips as he rested his head on Stacie's lap. "Hey, Eric, guess what? I'm going to be a dad. I'm going to be a dad."

Stacie smiled down at him. Tears dripped from her cheeks. "Yeah, you are."

"Congratulations," Eric said. "But, let's get the hell out of this water before we freeze our nuts off."

Stacie and Eric helped Paul out of the water. Then Paul assisted Eric. When all three were on the solid ice, they heard Blankenship half moaning and babbling out load. They all walked in silence toward the crippled man lying on the ice. Paul's hand bled some more as he squeezed his fist in anger while approaching

Blankenship. He'd never be able to unsee that arrogant smile on Blankenship's face as he tried to kill Stacie.

They arrived at the fallen man and stared down at him in disgust. Stacie picked up the ice spud again, determined to finish what she started.

"This is for killing my uncle you sonovabitch!"

Paul grabbed her arm and stopped her from bashing Blankenship's skull.

"No, Stacie." He pleaded. "You don't want to have to live with that decision."

Eric put his arm on Stacie's shoulder and consoled her. "Stacie…" Her eyes were focused on Blankenship.

"Stacie!" Eric shouted. He wanted her full attention. "Ernie's alive. He's okay."

"He's okay?" Stacie cried. "Uncle Ernie's alive?"

Eric nodded, and she turned and cried into Paul's shoulder. He squeezed her back, knowing how close they were to losing each other.

"Let's get the hell out of here," Paul whispered. Stacie nodded with her head against his chest.

They heard a gurgle and cough behind them, only to find Blankenship trying to turn his head enough to spit the blood that was accumulating in his throat.

"What about him?" Stacie asked.

Chapter 24 / *The Promise*

Paul, Stacie, and Eric stared at Blankenship, wondering what to do. Paul could see the fear in Blankenship's face, and that satisfied him. He wanted to pick up the shotgun and finish Blankenship, but he'd had enough violence for one day.

The bay was quiet now, except for the labored breathing coming from the paralyzed man lying on the ice. Then Paul heard the sqeaky boots approaching from behind him. He turned to see the Canadian limping toward them, fiery eyes that could have melted the ice, staring down at Blankenship. He struggled with every step and Paul forgave him for not appearing sooner. He was carrying the case that contained three million dollars and dropped it with a thump on the ice. The noise caused Blankenship to whirl his head to the side.

"Look at Mr. Tough Guy," the Canadian belittled. He squatted next to Blankenship's head, even though the pain of his wounds protested. "Super bodyguard, bad-ass black belt, can't be killed by anybody—taken out by a 120-pound pregnant woman."

The Canadian was enjoying the sight of the helpless man who tried to kill him.

"I made you a promise," the Canadian reminded Blankenship. "I promised you weren't getting off this ice alive." He grabbed Blankenship by the collar and dragged him with the last ounce of his strength toward the wrecked plane. He pulled so hard, that when he let go, Blankenship slid across four feet of wet ice. Blankenship briefly screamed, and then the river swallowed him.

The Canadian fell to his knees, exhausted, relieved, and remorseful.

"Who is he?" Stacie whispered. "Is he the man the police are looking for?"

"It's a long story. Let's go," Paul grabbed the arm of the Canadian. "Com'on. There's a retired doctor a few miles down the road. If you give him cash, he'll take care of you."

"I won't make it, Paul. You and your wife take this money and split it with Andy—I trust he'll know what to do." With that, he passed out on the ice.

Paul hustled across the ice to reach his Jet-sled, dumped all of his fishing gear out, and ran back to the Canadian. Eric grabbed the mechanic under the arms and Paul lifted his feet as they set him in the sled. Stacie explained what happened to Uncle Ernie as Paul and Eric dragged the sled. They moved as fast as they could across the bay and through the woods. Paul and Eric took turns dragging the sled loaded with the unconscious man. By the time they reached Garrison Road, they were all sweating from the exertion, despite their wet clothes.

Chapter 25 / *That Wasn't Blood*

Paul and Eric dragged the sled all the way to Haystack Rock. When they arrived, they found that Andy had walked from his cabin to the famous landmark. Andy was talking into his walkie-talkie, but no one was answering on the other end. Then he realized Paul wasn't dragging his fishing gear in the black sled. Andy peered into the sled and saw the lump of a man with blood all over him. The unconcious man's breathing was almost nonexistent and his eyes were closed.

"Is he dead?" Andy worried.

"Not yet, but, if we don't get him to a doctor soon, he will be."

"Doc Butler lives just down the road...," Andy started.

"That's what I was thinking," Paul offered. He was breathing heavily and had to force the words. "If we can get him there quickly, he just might make it, but he's lost a lot of blood."

Paul picked the silver case out of the icefishing sled and turned the tumblers. "What the hell year was that mustang? 1979?"

"Sixty-nine," Eric corrected.

Paul turned the four dials until the numbers read the correct year and the case popped open. He could sense Stacie's surprise and almost heard her mouth drop when she saw the contents of the case. Paul extracted one bundle of cash and reclosed the case. "This is for Doc Butler," he was holding the money up for Andy to see. "I'll give him this to take care of your brother-in-law and Jack's leg."

"I'll follow you down to Doc's as soon as I get my truck running," Andy stated.

Paul set the case of money at Andy's feet. "Take the money, Andy. Take the money and take care of your niece. We'll drop your brother-in-law off at Doc Butler's house, but he's your responsibility after that."

"We don't need the money," Eric said. "We have everything we need, and I think you do, too."

Andy picked up the case like it was a bomb. The responsibility seemed like such an enormous burden to the simple man. A burden that should not have been his. Andy wondered if he had gotten in over his head. Find the wrecked plane; that was his part of the plan. Now, he needed to take care of the wounded Canadian, keep the money safe, and drive them both to Mexico— all while avoiding police and who would be out looking for the wanted Canadian. He thought about dropping the case and just going home. Then, he thought about Sophia's smile and how long it had been since he had seen her or his sister.

"You could buy a new truck and drive to Mexico this week," Paul offered. "Three million dollars should go a long way."

"There are three million dollars in that case?" Stacie choked. "Where the hell did it come from?"

"From the plane that crashed on the ice. This guy took it down somehow because he knew it was on board. Things didn't quite work out the way he planned though."

"Drug money," Stacie said. Her eyes resumed their normal size and even squinted a little now. "I knew there was something fishy about that plane. The Border Patrol agents that did the inspection took a bribe to let it enter the country without an inspection."

"It stopped at the airport this morning?" Paul asked.

"Yes, it came from Canada."

"We know," Paul and Eric said in unison.

They were interrupted by the sound of an engine. Paul's truck came spinning around the corner with Jack behind the wheel, working the gas and brake with his left leg, while Ernie occupied the passenger side. He pulled up next to them and rolled down the window. "Let's get the hell out of here before someone else shows up looking for that plane. I think we've been shot at enough today."

Ernie exited the passenger side. Jack had bandaged his head, and he favored his bad hip. He only took a few steps, grabbed the open door for stability, and decided to wait for Stacie.

"Uncle Ernie!" Stacie broke from Paul and Eric and ran toward her uncle. She wrapped her arms around his neck. "I thought you were dead. I thought I'd lost you forever."

"Hell, it'll take more than a shot to the head to kill me, girl," he chuckled.

"But the blood…your chest was covered in blood. It was all over the snow."

She stared at his chest, still stained red.

Ernie grinned and pulled the metal flask from his snowmobile jacket. He rattled it to hear the small .22 caliber bullet still inside.

"That wasn't blood; it was cinnamon brandy," Ernie said. His grin turned to a scowl. "That bastard put a hole in my good flask. Your Aunt Marie bought me this for our second anniversary." He rubbed the pea size hole with his thumb, then showed Stacie how the hole was only on one side of the metal flask. "I got lucky, but damn, I sure could use a swig of that brandy right now."

Stacie admired his sentimentality and hugged him again; harder this time since she knew he had no wound to his chest. She could smell the brandy, and it transferred to her coat, but she didn't mind.

Andy interrupted. "You guys get out of here. I'll pick up your tip-ups and fishing gear and leave everything in your sleds. You can come back when you feel like it and pick them up. I'll leave everything on my front deck—in case I'm, uh, not around."

"We'll be back in a few days," Eric affirmed.

"Sounds good," Andy said. "I only ask for one favor…"

"Handing you three million dollars isn't enough?" Paul joked.

"Nope. Promise me that you guys will come back this spring and do some walleye fishing with me, hehe."

"You got it, Andy," Paul smiled, and reached out with his left hand since the right hand was bleeding from the bullet hole. Andy shook his hand and started the walk back to his cabin.

Paul and Eric hoisted the sled like a gurnie into the back of the Dodge. The Canadian's eyes opened for a moment, and Paul thought he heard him say, "Daddy's coming, Sophia." Stacie pulled a wool blanket off the backseat that Paul kept there in case the old truck broke down in the winter. She handed the blanket up to Paul, and he doubled it over and then covered the wounded Canadian. The edges of the blanket were tucked under the sled to ensure it stayed in place.

"It'll be a little cold on the ride, but it shouldn't take us more than 10 minutes," Paul advised, not sure if the Canadian was listening. He slammed the tailgate shut and climbed behind the wheel. Eric occupied the front passenger seat, while Stacie sat in the back between Ernie and Jack. Paul punched the accelerator pedal and spun the Dodge 180 degrees. Snow spit from the tires and they heard the sled in the back slide a little. Paul eased off the gas but raced down the road as fast as he dared go.

He began explaining everthing that had happened to Stacie and Ernie. He was talking as fast as he was driving, stopping every 30 seconds to catch his breath. He put his injured hand over the heater, allowing it to warm his blood and stave off the hypothermia. Eric copied his brother, but with both hands. When Paul finally finished telling the story of the day's events, everyone fell silent. They were exhausted and still in disbelief.

Paul thought about how lucky they all were to be alive. Then, he realized, luck had nothing to do with it. They were alive because they had each other; because they were family and they loved each other, and because they didn't give up on one another.

Paul peeked at Stacie in the rearview mirror. She was beautiful, even covered in blood and brandy. Her hair was wet and falling flat, and her makeup had worn off, but Paul thought she looked amazing. He couldn't believe how lucky he was to have such a strong, loving wife who would give him a child and be the best mother ever.

He didn't care that they had little money in their bank accounts or the fact that their credit was declining. He had everything he needed in this truck, and he'd do anything to protect it.

He thought about what he'd done to Blankenship—taking aim across the ice and putting a bullet into his arm, willing to shoot him dead if he had been a better marksman. The Canadian's advice stuck with him—how he spoke of reaching deep down within yourself, pushing past your fears to do what was necessary. That's what Paul would do from now on. That's what he would do for Stacie, himself, and his baby. He'd move, if necessary, to find work. He'd take a shitty job, or he'd start his own business.

He was going to reach deep.

He was going to make things work.

Chapter 26 / *The Investigation*

It had been over a week since the plane crash was investigated by the authorities. No one could explain how the Beechcraft ended up in the Raquette River or what kind of device could have done so much damage to the plane.

They never found the Canadian's homemade drone. Cordelia was blown into pieces when she exploded. The debris fell into the blackberry bushes. The stalks of the plants were an inch thick and covered with thorns strong enough to pierce winter clothing, and walking through them was impossible, so the search party that was investigating the scene avoided the area completely.

The plane's pilot—still floating in the cockpit—was identified as Ozzy Sullivan, and the missing passenger was presumed to be lost under the ice. A dive team wouldn't find Blankenship for several more weeks. His autopsy report listed his cause of death to be from drowning—drowning because he broke his neck in the crash. The body was decomposed enough that the coroner identified the bullet holes as wounds from the bomb that destroyed the plane.

Evidence of Andy's involvement with the scene was covered by a snow squall that hit the area that same night. Heavy snow covered his tracks that led away from the crash site. The snow also covered up any evidence that the Marten brothers had been at the scene.

The official report stated that a saboteur had planted a bomb onboard the private plane. The motive was unclear, but it was assumed that a disgruntled mechanic was to blame. The mechanic fled the country, killing Travis "Moonie" Swamp who assisted him crossing the border, and was at large somewhere in New York. The news channels reported him as a homicidal outlaw, a senseless killer, and extremely dangerous—and whatever else they could come up with to entertain an audience.

Paul cursed the news channels and the papers. They didn't truly know anything about the Canadian or his motivation.

Stacie insisted that Ernie be taken to the emergency room, where he made up a story about his head injury, telling the doctors that it was caused when his dog, Alphie, jumped up on him while rabbit hunting. The dog inadvertently knocked the rifle and it fired, striking him in the head and causing him to spill his flask of brandy. He was released after a catscan and a few pain killers, then went home with Aunt Marie.

Paul, Jack, and Eric drove up to Andy's cabin after the investigation was closed. Andy was nowhere to be found, but just like he promised, the Marten's fishing gear was neatly organized in the two sleds that were left behind. The sleds were parked on Andy's porch, mostly protected from daily snowfall, except when the wind blew the white flakes horizontally.

Jack opened the front door of Andy's cabin and walked inside. It was cold inside—the woodstove had been shut down for days, maybe longer.

"Think he'll make it…to Mexico?" Jack asked.

"I hope so," Paul replied. "If not, well, I guess he'll be a very rich man."

"Until he does something stupid and gets arrested," Jack laughed.

They were interrupted by Eric, "Hey guys?" He was pawing through his fishing gear to be sure everything was his.

"What is it?"

"You might want to check your pack baskets," Eric called.

Paul and Jack exited Andy's cabin. Eric was holding a stack of one-hundred dollar bills.

"It was in the bottom of my basket."

"That dumbass," Jack said. "He should have taken the entire amount."

Paul and Jack searched their baskets, and sure enough, they, too, found a wad of bills. They rushed to count the stacks and found that Andy had left them each 20 thousand dollars.

Epilogue

The old truck bounced down the dirt road, rattling like a bag of empty paint cans that made it difficult to hear each other speak. The driver was hard on the clutch and ground the gears with a terrible sound which reminded the passengers in the back of a garbage disposal. They were tucked away among boxes and crates of medical supplies that shifted occasionally and reduced their hiding space within the cargo area. Dust poured in from a large crack in the floorboard, and the smell of exhaust was nauseating.

The driver slowed the truck, the garbage disposal grinding on and off as he down shifted and finally stopped. The deisel diesel engine continued to rattle, and the two passengers could hear the driver speaking to someone in Spanish.

The driver and the man outside laughed about something. The truck lurched forward, gears ground again, and they began to accelerate. The speed of the truck blew more dust into the cargo box and covered the passengers and the medical boxes. After another 30 minutes of traveling, they slowed and came to rest again. This time, the engine was killed, and the driver exited the Mitsibishi cargo truck. The back door rolled upward, and the fresh air cooled the interior slightly.

The driver climbed into the back, pulled on a dolly, and rolled a large crate toward the back of the truck. The Canadian and Andy arose from their hiding place behind the crate.

"Are we here?" Andy asked the driver.

"Sí, yes. We are in Mexico. You are safe to come out," the driver assured them. He stepped off the back of the truck and kept his eyes on the two stowaways. "I can bring you no further, Mr. Andy."

The Canadian had a green canvas bag slung over his shoulder. He limped forward and struggled to step down from the truck. He looked around to verify they had reached Mexico, but the morning sun wasn't bright enough to be sure. "This is Mexico?" He asked just to be sure.

"This is, yes. We crossed the border 30 minutes back," The driver said as he pointed back down the road.

The Mexican driver was short and fit, but his belly carried an extra 25 pounds. The sides of his hair were gray, and his face was like leather from years in the sun.

"Boy, thanks for doing this, Charlie," Andy smiled at the driver. "I know you were taking a big risk, hehe."

"Where are you going to go, Mr. Andy?" Charlie asked.

"We're going to find my sister and my niece. Haven't seen them in a few years."

"You need to go back to the U.S. after that?" Charlie asked.

"Not for a while—maybe in a month or two. There might be four of us next time."

The Canadian removed the canvas bag and set it on the back of the truck, then extracted a bundle of cash from the bag and handed it to Andy, who passed it to Charlie.

"Here's the rest of your money, buddy," Andy offered as he handed Charlie five thousand dollars. Charlie looked at the money in disbelief. They'd already given him five thousand at the start of the trip, and now he was ten thousand dollars richer. The side of the bag flopped over to reveal the rest of the cash that filled the duffle. Greed krept up Charlie's back and consumed him. He felt his heart begin to race as adrenaline spiked inside his veins. His next reaction was a surprise, even to himself. His hand retrieved a Browning BDA-380 revolver that had been tucked behind his back. He pointed the barrel at the Canadian and Andy, swinging side to side with jittery movements.

The Canadian studied the gun for a moment, noticing the rust and pits in its nickel finish. The grip was small, more suitable for a woman's hand, but it seemed just right for the Mexican weilding it with a shakey right hand. The four-inch barrel was engraved, but not professionally, and the frame was small, which made it perfect to tuck in one's belt. The middle-aged Mexican must have had it behind his back, tucked into his jeans. He had his finger on the trigger, but the nervous man who'd brought them across the border forgot to switch the safety button into the firing position. Charlie's voice shook more than his hand.

"Please, set the bag…set the bag down on the dirt," he directed his request with the pistol.

"Whoa, whoa, whoa, Charlie," Andy startled. "I thought we had a deal. You smuggle us across the border, we give you 10 grand."

Charlie blinked hard. He wiped his sweaty forehead with the back of his arm.

"You have no idea what I've been through to get this money," the Canadian fumed. His voice had dropped a few octives, and his eyes went cold. He glared at Charlie without blinking.

"The price just went up, amigo," Charlie replied. "You leave money here and start walking that way," he was pointing East, but really didn't care where they went. "Leave the bag, imbécil. Maybe you get lucky and get more someday." This time he spoke directly to the Canadian.

The Canadian sighed, zipped the bag closed and took a few steps toward Charlie. The bag dropped with a thud as it hit the ground. The Canadian's stare was unwavering.

"You sure you want this money?" the Canadian challenged. "You sure you're willing to reach deep within yourself and find the strength to take it?"

Charlie seemed confused by the question. Of couse he wanted it. Of course he had the strength—he had the friggin' gun. That was all the strength he needed. He smirked and reached down for the bag. It was heavier than he had anticipated but hoisted it to his left shoulder with little effort. The weight set him slightly off balance. The money was his now.

The Canadian's hands moved in a blur, timed perfectly with a head feint to the right. Before Charlie could realize what was happening, the Canadian's right hand came left, grabbing the slide of the pistol. His left forearm came up, as the right hand pulled the gun down. The force of the burly forearm against the thin wrist broke the pistol from Charlie's hand instantly, and a half-second later Charlie was staring down the barrel of his own gun.

*** THANK YOU ***

Stay up to date with future books from Terry Paul Fisher by visiting his website and signing up. You will receive occasional announcements, free stuff, and updates on future books. Your email address will never be sent spam, and no information will ever be sold to a third party—promise.

www.terrypaulfisher.com

Your support is greatly appreciated.
Please, consider leaving a review for Depth Finder on Amazon.

Reviews are crucial for independent authors and assist us by letting other readers know if this title is a good fit for them.